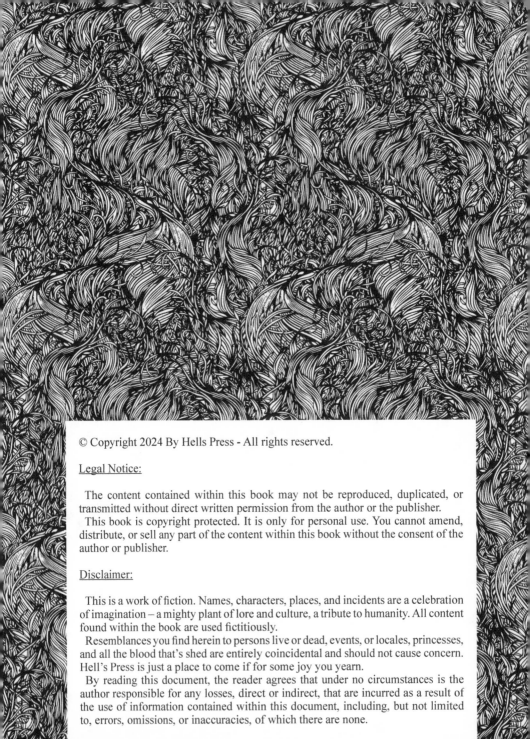

ISBN: 978-1-7381322-8-7

DARK & TWISTED

FAIRY TALES FOR ADULTS

A CLASSIC COLLECTION OF DARK, DERANGED, AND
INTRIGUING FAIRY TALES RETOLD

COUNT FATHOM

HELLS PRESS

TABLE OF CONTENTS

This is for you, the tired, the poor, the huddled masses yearning to breathe free, the reader with a sweet tooth, or an odd proclivity. We yearn for entertainment, and I'm here for you to serve. A tale to pass away an hour, if you like a moral curve. What some see as bent is straight, if you have eyes like mine. I see a house that tilts a bit, and I think that it's just fine.

Our Fairie Tales are watered down, as at our pearls we clutch. All our pigments turn to brown, lest we offend too much. I've come with colours from the sun to wash our stagnant skies, and clear up all the misconceptions, fibs and outright lies. See us for the first time now, as we really are. We're wicked, good and in between, some are quite bizarre. Even I, a moral grey, do think they've gone too far.

Preface

Fie! This is the first. It's not the worst and nor is it the best. You enter now upon a path that proves a moral test. Jack is something of a host, he'll take you to your seat. He'll read by heart a wine list, and he'll advertise the meat. A joke, a pun, a shoulder touch, a hypnotizing guile. Beneath a spell he'll put you, unbeknownst to you the while. Once you're set and comfortable, you'll think you've found your place. But others form a queue behind to smack you in the face.

These are tales you've heard before, but not the way you thought. The cook is quite creative adding spices to the pot. Hot, you say, or bitter. Some say sweet, or tough to chew. Pleasure comes in many forms, is it just right for you? Promises I will not make, for I am me, not you. I'm in the kitchen cooking, curating your meal. You'll feast, and when it's done you'll know you don't know how to feel. Full you'll be, with images, with thoughts and shock and fun. The food in this establishment would wet a pious nun. So settle back, relax a bit, and taste a hot cross bun.

JACK AND THE BEANSTALK

Through vale and valley, glen and gorge, fen and meadow and plain, as scattered as they may be varied, are all the crawling, walking, wading, warbling creatures of creation going about their doings indifferent to one another. And among all this criss-crossing life, at odds and evens, are the intersections of interaction, the interlocutions, the touching of one to another to commune, to resolve, or to entertain. How glorious the possibilities!

I will serve before you a particularly tasty treat. In this case you might think him a kind of logger. But you would be wrong. You see him there, snap snap, up a tree, right near the top. That's what loggers do, isn't it? But where's his saw? He hasn't one. He has a gob of a bag, but it's near empty. He's gathering something there. Are they nests? Why yes they are! That's the nest of a curlew. Lucky for you my ornithological competence, for the curlew is a rare bird and becoming rarer by the day. Maybe that's why Jack's bag is near empty.

The setting sun spreads marmalade across the sky, and lickety snap, what a funny chap, Jack skates down the tree like a bow legged puppet, boot spikes tap dancing down the bark to the conductor of fate, a mysterious maestro manipulating those who will submit. It's some time before our new friend reaches the threshold of his home, a small flip of farm land with a host of buried ancestry interred. A bond and a trust with their plot, nourished with generations of blood. Each corpse was a sacrifice to the kami, the jinn, the leprechaun of the land. Jack and his mother will soon join them.

Jack's mother took a long look in the bag Jack plopped on the kitchen table. Then she stuck her whole head inside. Jack heard her sobbing in there. "No, mother! I feel it! The tide of fortune is turning in our favour. The curlew told me so. Tomorrow will be better. We'll have enough nests for some salt. Then you'll see. We'll have the family affairs right soon enough."

With the bag still over her head, mother stood stalk straight facing Jack, silent for a moment. An order barked sharply at Jack, with the authority of an menacing index finger to back it up, "Go early to market with the cow. Sell her for what you can get. Bring food and the rest of the money home to me."

Up Jack got, beating the birds to breakfast, the following morn and fetched a lead for Rowina. Jack had drunk rivers of milk from the old girl since he was just a wee lad. But mother did the milking, and Rowina would nip at Jack had she the chance. Jack swore to mother about the cow, accusing the fiendish beast of cursing him with the evil eye, even going so far as to claim the steady decline of the family affairs dates back to her purchase. In fact, the cow had, indeed, been jealous of the coddling Jack received as a child, and harboured a long standing grudge against him. She was a shrewd conniver, that one, and Jack kept a distance until the impulse to torment the old lady became too strong.

Giving her a good hard slap on her bony ass, Jack and Rowina marched off down the forest path suffering some emotional confusion. Several years hence, with her eyesight failing and her hair falling out in the twilight of her life, Rowina would still find joy in reminiscence, her periodic spontaneous malevolence towards this boy who grew into a man before her very eyes. A disgrace of a man, in her opinion, always in his dreams, never his mind on where he is and what he is doing. She spit and they walked on.

Jack had not a thought in his head. But then one hit him. And he hopped up straddling Rowina backwards, erupting in gay laughter at her expense. The old girl lurched her ass against an oak, an overhanging limb knocked Jack's noggin, and Jack tumbled to the ground in a daze. A fog befell him, when just then a little old waddler bent over, brushing a bushy grey beard chin to forehead across Jack's face.

Jack was bleary. He propped himself between oak and elbow, and tried to follow the gesticulating dance and strange foreign accents of the lively little fellow before him. In a dazzling pirouette, the green dwarf flourished forth in a low bow, palm extended entreating Jack to examine. Three beans were therein.

Submitting to the beckon of fathomless fate, Jack's hand received the proffered beans. Jack fell back once more in a daze, clutching at his banged brains in pitiful pain, whimpering himself into a slumber in due time. Under a spell of darkness the mind is unshackled from beastly activity. Into the immense unknown, carried in currents through channels and canals and over stormy black seas sails a slumbering something, unencumbered and free. But the body butts in and the spell is undone and we wake enslaved once again. Up Jack got to a sunset, puzzled at the loss of the day.

Jack is elated! He is the saviour of his family's fortune, for clever Jack had outwitted them all and converted that sick old cow into three magical beans. Think of the tearful penitence of his mother, he, Jack, all powerful before her. Her at this feet, on her knees in obeisance and gratitude to the shrewd unfathomed intellect of her great son, Jack!

Jack skipped across water to the very door of his home, bursting with inner pride and joy. For love of God, he wished he'd had a trumpeter, or a flugelist, or a cockerel to announce his grand arrival. "Mum! I've settled the family affairs for all time. Bow before me you filthy swine!", and his hand thrust magnificently towards the heavens, heralding the magic beans.

"You've sold the cow for a handful of beans! You rascal, child! I'll beat the life out of you for this!" swore his mother, in disgust and outrage. A slight woman, and starved gaunt by years of privation, Jack's mother yet wielded a determined, ferocious temper when her wrath was summoned. Switch in hand, the spritely red faced witch chased Jack out the room and about the yard, whipping him merci-lessly, and, in his efforts to protect himself from the onslaught, Jack flailed the precious beans he knew not where.

Exhausted, panting, sweat pooling at her chin, and soaking the collar of her shirt, mother took to a chair to recover, threatening, "you just wait until your father comes home!", and Jack sighed with relief. They had heard nothing about his father for two years, since he had been conscripted to soldier in the king's army, against an obscure enemy in far flung lands. Mother was now in tears. Both retired to their rooms without a word, and starving, as they had noth-ing to eat.

Jack felt hard done by, and clenched his fists in resentment and wounded honour for some time before drifting off into the land of the elves. An uneasy sleep, haunted by the goblins and ghouls of the other world and their horrendous yips and moans, before coming to at what should have been the break of dawn.

But on this magical morning, looking east, the sun was nowhere to be seen. The entirety of the fiery eye was eclipsed by three enormous braided green stalks, stretching from the nourishing black earth right into the ephemeral heavens, beyond the sight of man. Jack staggered outside, arched his head back scouring the skies for an end to the magnificent growth, bopped his head against his ass and tumbled over into the dirt. An inquisitive piglet ambled by and sniffed enthusiastically at the prone Jack, tickling the young man with its eager pumping snout.

Jack, being nimble, hopped to his feet, bent his head back once again, but knew better this time when to rein it in and didn't tumble over. Far enough that his mouth caverned open, his sight line parallel to gravity, and, yes, it happened again. His head hit his ass and he tumbled over onto the dirt, Betsy nosing pig slobber over him, moisturizer for young Jack's face. Jack hopped up.

Jack felt an inner fire ignite. Tinder to kindling to log to coal in just moments, a determination Jack had never felt the likes of before. Jack looked up a third time, and was able to remain for some time staring into the heavenly realm. He felt a wave of accomplishment ripple through, his hair an electric tingle, and his flesh bubbled like an untended pot. He wouldn't tumble over. His beans were magic. And he was the saviour of the family affairs. Jack thrust a fist skyward.

Quite sure, confident, in fact, doubts dismissed as ridiculous, Jack immediately prepared to climb to the top of this marvellous monstrosity. The fruits of his finest financial philosophy finalized to fantastic satisfaction. This stalk was fortune's hand reaching down to him, fate bending to offer him all his merry heart may desire, were he only to take that chance.

Without waiting to wake mother, Jack pranced into action, snatching the gob of a bag with three final curlew nests, some string and a knife to help manage the transportation of all his hopes and dreams. Strapping on and lacing up his climbing boots, Jack attacked his task with all the enthusiasm of the unrelenting optimist. He was a good tall tree up in a snap, and two in two more. Snap snap. He kept that pace up for a snap and eight more, but from thence he slowed markedly, taking four snaps, then ten for a tree of fair height.

What a marvel!, thought Jack, as he climbed the bare root. For it started to sprout, first sparsely, then densely, the most varied and glorious of mother earth's fruit. Up up, up the day passed, stopping once for a bite. Then he hung his bag gently as a bed for the night. On and on went our Jack, his provisions ran low, but the fruit on the root were beginning to grow, to fabulous sizes until, near the end, the fruit that he found shamed a hippo's rear end.

The first three nights in the bag were the worst. A flock of sparrow or finch would often flutter by, ever curious as to Jack's intentions. They would spit and gossip the most ludicrous nonsense about fairy kingdoms and sugar candy mountains and cavernous mining dwarves and the fires of dragons and haunts of despicable evil. On days four and five visits by flock were no longer common, Jack might spend a meal chatting with a condor or a vulture. The one had much to say about the state of affairs, but wouldn't go far in politics, as he lacked all conviction in his proposed remedies, asign of intelligence if you ask me.

Jack suspected the other was waiting for him to fall. The vulture might peck at Jack's socks, claiming to unburden him of a briar, or it might bump Jack as he climbed, pardon having forgotten his spectacles. The vulture, however, was a rhetorician of tremendous and frightening ability.

"I am despised, for I feed on the flesh of the dead. My handsome, splendid features are unappreciated. I glisten with secretion, adapted for my most perfect survival, and I am accused of being unclean. The herd of bleating sheep you consider enlightened is led by nothing more than appetite."

Here the vulture, gaped wide his beak and snapped shut again, a shade from Jack's cheek.

"You scramble over one another, worse than rats escaping a fire. Towards what end? So you can sit atop the mountain of struggling flesh. Together you could accomplish so much, were you in tune. How can you be, when you have undermined nature's greatest gift – the survival of the fittest. The weak have been dragged forward generation by generation through the greed of your state, as workers create wealth. Those that would naturally die off now pollute your stream beyond hope."

The tightly squinting vulture hack hacked out a phlegmatic squirt of sticky spit, and dropped it onto the world below.

"You reward greed, self-interest, deception, and insincerity. Your species is a disease, You have poisoned our world, and I am disgusted with you. I wait for your death, Jack, with great anticipation. I will enjoy tearing your guts from your body and spreading them wide for my amusement. Your suffering and humiliation will atone for the sins of your kind."

When he had climbed high enough to leave the vulture below, Jack was immensely relieved.

After a week of nights in the bag, only the rarest and noblest of animals, true philosophers, were to be met. A majestic crane spent much of the second week visiting Jack regularly, between feedings. They were above the highest peak at this point, and the air was stranglingly thin. The winds at the higher altitudes were terrifying. Luckily, Jack had neglected to cut his nails for some time past, and was able to latch himself to the now thinning beanstalk securely. At such times as the winds forced Jack into one spot, the crane, a benevolent creature and sociable as well, would encircle Jack in a wing cocoon, where they would whisper to one another, sometimes for hours, until the fates allowed Jack to continue his climb.

"What you see before you is a mirage," the crane had said, "you are incapable of perceiving the true nature of matter, and the subtle tangle of woven forces that comprise the fabric of our reality. You live in a world of shadow. Within a very narrow beam of visible light, you say you see all. You are wrong. All your technological wizardry, while clever, is hopelessly limited and will end in a paradox of multiplicity. The forces of the higher dimensions are immeasurable from your relative position."

Jack felt not lost in the presence of the crane, despite the inevitability of his ignorance revealed. "But don't lose heart! All of us have enough. We can feel the harmonic pulse of life propagating through land, air, and sea, and, in fact, space and time. You must blend your life sound into the great symphony of all. And you, Jack, have done so."

"Destiny guides the heart. Every time you have submitted to her call, you have thrust a fist triumphantly into the air. You are following strings of fate, as you should, through a web far too grand in scale for your comprehension. When we resist, we deviate, we encounter obstruction and difficulty. Your stubborn free will is an debilitating impediment to your natural progress. I shed tears for the tragic fate of humanity. Such gifts squandered on shit throwing apes."

Here the crane left off for some time, staring into the unobscured nothingness, swaddled in the howling of eternity.

"Am I to gain my treasure? My reward for my acquiescence? Will I be rich as a king?"

"Yes, Jack. Your reward awaits you in the heavenly spheres. I will leave you now. Follow, don't lead."

And with that the crane flew off into the mist. The mist? Jack was enveloped in a suffocating greyness. He was overcome, momentarily, by a shiver of terror, and clutched desperately to the stalk, eyes clenched, whispering for mother and mercy.

Some minutes passed, and Jack felt a little silly, his fingers dug in two knuckles deep, choking the plant with his thighs, and the sweat of fear pouring out of him. The great beanstalk carried on upward for only four snaps more, before dwindling to a fine tip. Unclenching his eyes to a surprise, Jack was but the width of a man from solid ground. Where did that come from? Jack was puzzled. The mist had dissipated. Far beneath his feet, clouds frolicked in a merry dance, moving from partner to partner in blended motifs of dissonance and harmony. A sun bathed field lay before Jack, rolling some ways before breaking upon the bulwarks of a magnificent castle.

Jack hopped off the stalk into a forest of grass, each blade his height. This was the land of giants. How was it that from the crane to the vulture, to all their silly little cousins, all the creatures he had met had spoken knowingly of this wondrous land? Jack, of course, had heard stories about ogres and trolls, and had conversed at length with animals since his youngest memories. But this land of giants, cloaked in cloud among the heavens was beyond his imagination.

Letting his heart lead the way, Jack began with a few uncertain steps through the grass forest. Each step brought confidence, and soon Jack and his heart were racing, the blades around him bending away from the compression of the air in front of a hard -charging Jack. In this land of the gods, Jack himself had changed. He felt strong. He felt fast. He felt he was still himself, but the reliable laws of nature had altered mysteriously. He felt torrents coursing through him. Jack was immersed in an ocean of chaotic energy, which would channel through him as a river through a narrow canyon. Rapids of energy roared through Jack. Bug eyed wild, Jack zigged, zipped, and zoomed in a violent and erratic pattern known only to his soul.

And he did not go unnoticed. He was a riotous disturbance for countless residents. A ladybug, big as Jack's head, was frightened out of her wits, spun dizzy, knocked against a stick, and fell belly up in the mud. A caterpillar, munching comfortably mid way up and through a tasty blade, when Jack came storming along, breaking the blade with the force of his outstretched arm. The caterpillar fell in the most undignified and humiliating fashion, causing an outbreak of hilarity amongst the fleas and crickets and mites and hoppers nearby. And far above, within the top turret of this giant's castle, a not so fair lady spied young Jack's performance, and approved.

From deep in the bowels of the cursed dungeons came a growling big bass howl.

"Fee! Fi! Fo! Fum! I smell the blood of an Englishman. Be he alive or be he dead, I'll grind his bones to make my bread."

"Henry, you keep your filthy remarks to yourself for the rest of today. How often must I suffer these ranting outbursts of yours? This morning he was French. And they come up so irregularly, that I'll not tolerate having you stir up a hornets's nest in the castle every time your intuition whispers in your ear. If we have a visitor, you'll catch up with him soon enough. They'll be coming into the castle, after all. Express your enjoyment in silence, my dear."

She was a booming tenor. Sweet in the higher register, melodious in the low. Her sound reverberated round and down the medieval stone, and the towers sung like pipe organs in answer to the mistress. Henry, that ape, slow as he spoke, had adopted a poor posture from a young age. It was never corrected, and led to permanent muscular dystrophy, an hunched burly brutish giant, with horror and doom in his voice.

Meanwhile, Jack zoomed past the manicured garden beds, raised and inset at just Jack's height, past the spitting fountain, choreographed to some of classical music's finest, across an immense drawbridge, of wood thick as thrice the length of a man, through a closed, but porous grated iron gate, and straight up to Henry's humongous castle doors. Jack was quite small enough to squeeze under, like a blade of grass himself, and was soon zooming to his heart's desire in and out, around and under, through and between for all the treasures to be found therein. And he found his way, at last, to the top of the tallest staircase in the tallest turret of the tallest tower. And he met Magogola.

Of frightening size, one step could crush a man, Jack fixated on her enormous feet.

"Hello, my dear. I see you there." The slow melody milked out of the giant. Jack was entranced. "And where might you be from?"

Jack was stunned, but the rivers still surged through him, propelling, enforcing action. "I'm Jack! I climbed the magic beanstalk. I followed my heart to my treasure, and it has brought me to you!"

Jack scrambled up a calf, under a loose frock blindly weaseled through an elastic waistband, up and hugged her heart tight. The proustian spell fell like confetti after a pulse or two and Jack scampered down in a snap and three more. "You fine little fellow! I will give you all your heart desires. Come back to Magogola!"

Jack, again submitting to the now unstoppable force of fate, dashed straight for her toes. She shrieked as he spun and twirled and fished under and over those pot bellied pigsies. She howled and moaned in delight, and shook with an explosion of ecstasy, as Jack settled down, snuggling into a hammock between Lucy and Consuela, as he called them, pigs two and three. Magogola was thrilled with her new friend. She kept him as a pet.

Henry was grouchy about the situation. He would eat this man one day, that was understood, and reaffirmed by his other half, his sister, and his wife. Their giant life cycle is peculiar, in that an egg is fertilized once in a lifetime through perfect affection, and bears two offspring of differing sex, bound to renew their kind. The older generation die off as the younger mature. Henry and Magogola were destined to bear an egg of this kind. He, being such a brute, failed to excite her emotions, and both feared much time might pass before they could fulfill their duty. Jack was tolerated, as he clearly entertained his sister, and lifted her spirits. And he had generously endowed three curlew nests upon his hosts, considered a delicacy among the giants. But along with Henry's appetite, his jealousy would grow.

Jack rode Magogola everywhere. All over the house, and on the furniture, in practically every room, out in the garden, further afield in the trees, along magical paths, sharing with one another the splendours of life. A friendship quickly developed into a heartfelt bond, a touching of souls, and having once shared of the same waters, will forever be part of one another. Magogola felt her heart's desires fulfilled.

In return, she would lavish Jack in comfort and ease. Lobster so large that it could threaten an armada would be served meat extracted and set using the tail for a bowl, a bowl the size of a small lake for Jack. Then for supper, steak from a beast that could devour a rainforest would sit like stacked mattresses on the table, as Jack scurried around taking tiny nibbles hardly noticeable. One impulsive day, while Jack and Goggy, as he now referred to her, lay in the grass by a river, his mistress removed from her purse a lovely golden harp, but of a size suitable to Jacl's world below. The harp began to play a light lovely lilting little libretto accompaniment all by itself. Jack was agog. Zoom! Jack was off on a tear through the blades once again, in joyous celebration, fist thrust skyward.

Goggy was in tears of laughter, and gave the harp outright to Jack as a memento of her affection. Jack spun dizzy till he dropped, and had to be carried home in the bag with the harp, which was placed in Jack's private space, in a corner of Goggy's room. This was rather rash, as the harp, among countless other items, had been inherited by each generation of their kind over millennia. And the origins of the harp are a mystery, but I dare think Orpheus. Now it was little Jack's. Henry would not approve.

Over time Goggy came to truly love our little Jack. One purple crimson painted evening, the curtains were drawn close around our soul mates. Assumption, conjecture, and slander will tell of what was shared between them that night. But we know that Jack emerged with a very special creature as reward. Goggy gave Jack her goose, again an inheritance long ago from below. This goose shat gold eggs, one a day, a magical, fabled creature, and the undoing of empires, now sat next to the harp in Jack's corner.

Several weeks hence, Goggy began to show signs that she was with egg. And Henry caught on.

"Fee! Fie! Fo! Fum! Englishman for crust and crumb. When I find Jack, he's good and dead! I'll grind his bones to make my bread. And wash him down with fog and rum!"

Bullish Henry bounced off walls while cornering at alarming speed, over and over again, the very castle itself began to tremble. And he didn't stop, charging from room to room, thundering bloody murder as he went. Creatures for leagues around took shelter at the frightful eruption. Irate and irrational, Henry went to blazes and back, while Magogola had time to secure an escape for her beloved.

Jack was terrified. Goggy rushed in, glistening and breathless. A wordless panic gripped them. Then Jack held up his string. He tied it around his body, and the other end to his gob of a bag, now carriage for the harp and the well mannered goose. Jack hopped into his toe hammock. The fear ebbed, and confidence took hold. They were off.

Only steps from the door to the castle, and crashing in ferocious and wild comes unhinged Henry. He seizes Magogola at the elbows in a vice and lifts her clear from the stones.

"I'll have that English rat tonight!" roars Henry, frantic. Then with a broken miserable melancholy howl, "Where is he?"

Henry dropped Goggy plop on the stones, and off he went in a sobbing rage.

Goggy took a breath to steady her wounded heart, and moved off intent, through the humongous castle doors, beneath the raised grated iron gate, over the immense drawbridge, past the spitting fountain, and beyond the manicured garden beds. Goggy stood at the very precipice of her world, and the tears began to fall.

Jack would be saved, but lost forever. But forever was not so very long for her, as she knew. She had to fend for herself from such a young age that she could not remember her parents beyond their horrifying lifeless bodies, pushed out into the river. The same would happen to her. So she let her little Jack descend upon the magic vine, connecting the upper and lower worlds, with confused and crippling emotions.

Jack made haste, but was inconvenienced by the cumbersome weight of his wares. Seventy thousand seven hundred and seventy seven snaps later, from the heavens far above, in the bluest of all blue days came the vile, thundering quake, "Fee! Fie! Fo! Fum!"

Submitting to the summons of fate disguised in instinct, Jack pulls the knife from its sheath, and hacks away in a mad fever of panicked attack. Within minutes this still immature part of the vine succumbed to Jack's insanity, and a river of twisting green stalk rushed past. A booming vowel blew on the wind from above, sharper, louder, a crescendo, then Doppler shifting smoothly through the low registers, and ending in a deep reverberating pulse that shivered through Jack tip to toe. So fast as to be nearly unseen, Henry fell to his death far below in the world of men, hidden in the deepest forest, soon grown over in a thick carpet of moss and lichen, and never yet recovered.

Jack held close to the stalk, wearied and weak. Weaker by the snap. Above, the richness and wonders of the heavens dizzied Jack's mind further, and he resolved to let the matter lie until he could deliberate at leisure upon such glory. Jack couldn't help but look one last long moment more into the infinite possible, thrust his fist triumphantly towards the gods, when who should fly by, out of the fine blue, but his friend the crane, tipping his wings in greeting and congratulations, giving Jack a loop and diminishing into the horizon, where all things meet.

Descending ever faster, Jack fevered with excitement, his pride swelling dangerously, let his imagination run amok within his mind. "Mother! I am the saviour of the family affairs! Bow beneath me, you wretched swine!" Like a dart from a dark cloud, a blurred bullet of a bird burst by, snipping violently at the string securing Jack's plunder. Stunned, Jack in a second saw fall, and forever lost, the favours of fortune, as they had come. Miraculously. A hacking vulture guffaw rippled into time, behind a final song from our goose, svelte and sleek, that believed she was a swan.

Jack gazed down now upon the world, the vales and dales, the field and furrow, the fog and frost and sadness and death, marbled mountains a licentious tease, a peek up mother earth's skirt , the glassy glacial melt water forging valley into the hardest rock, pastures and paddies and ponies and princes and paupers alike, and the fickle fingers of fate, whether an agent of conscious intent or a finite riddle one might calculate, grieve Jack must and grieve Jack did, as down the stalk and into history he finally and forever slid.

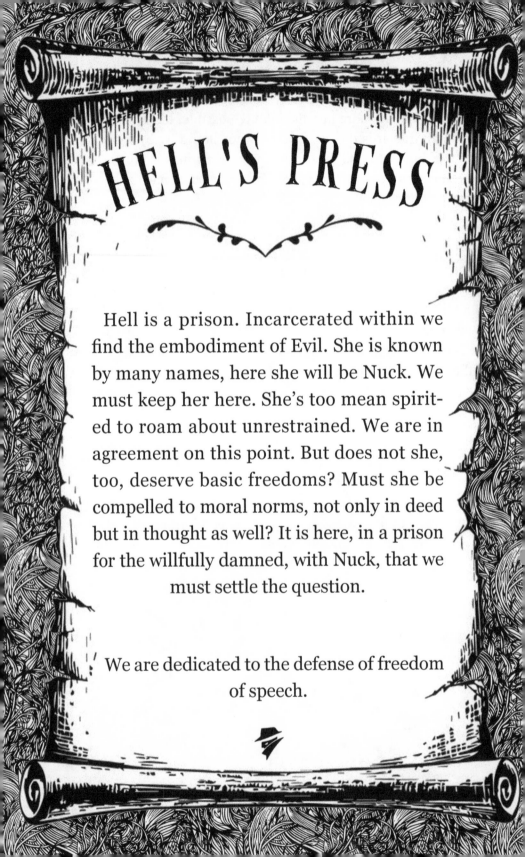

HELL'S PRESS

Hell is a prison. Incarcerated within we find the embodiment of Evil. She is known by many names, here she will be Nuck. We must keep her here. She's too mean spirited to roam about unrestrained. We are in agreement on this point. But does not she, too, deserve basic freedoms? Must she be compelled to moral norms, not only in deed but in thought as well? It is here, in a prison for the willfully damned, with Nuck, that we must settle the question.

We are dedicated to the defense of freedom of speech.

Preface

You've been through one already and now you're back for more. But that was just a taste, a morsel, ornament, décor. You're wondering now if that's the end, what else I have in store.

You've met our Jack, his giant love, and you thought good and right. If love is true, it overcomes the difference in their height. It's time to send a shot your way and give you quite a fright.

I'm not the man you think I am, we've only just begun. I'll not allow you think me well, ideals must be undone. I'm loud and brash and full of scorn, I'll burn you like the sun.

Here comes spite and hatefulness in stories two and three. Not from me, but from the hoard, who won't forgive a barren moral tree. I disdain their righteous sense of staunch morality.

My Heroines are beautiful, but victims they are not. Nor are they models for the children, chaste and pure, that stuff is rot. They are people, they are animals, their lives are tied in knots.

These women are not helpless, they just do the best they can. They look out for themselves, they plot, they scheme, they form a plan. And yes, it's true, their path to fortune sometimes leads them to a man.

Heroines they are to me, for them I have respect. Herein a moral looseness is not counted a defect. Self-reliance is the measure, for their very lives they must protect.

Anyway you'll hate me, that I'm sure of, that I know. You'll hate until you shiver, til you're hot enough to glow. Enough foreplay now, you're ready for it, let's begin the show.

BO PEEP

"Bethany Ann Olivia John." Those were the last words of Marshal Peep, coal miner by trade and dead at 26. They were to be the names of his only child, a girl, one last final insult from god, as he saw things, before his soul detached forever from his mortal shell.

She was a precocious child, forever asking why of whomever was nearest. She certainly didn't intend to annoy people, and nor did she, at least the men. An adorable child, treated kindly and thinking all received the same. In adolescence she was aware, as men would clutch their hearts and sigh at the sight of her. By maturity Betsy Peep, whom everyone called Bo, was at the height of her influence, and she knew it too. It had been years already since she had paid for anything. Shopkeeps would fill a bag for her and scurry her off before the wife returned, invariably justifying their charity for not so little Bo with a flippant "Her father's dead and her mother's a drunk whore with one foot in the grave."

Which was true. Her mother put the other foot in just then, leaving Bo orphaned at the end of her formative years, but not without some sage parting advice with which Bo could secure her position in life, "You're dumb as a toad, Bo. Marry rich or you'll starve once your looks go." Bo, not such a fool as to think herself a genius, was still a little hurt by this final presumption of her mother. But she took the advice to heart, like a sensible girl would, and this story will tell you how she went about it.

Though she would follow the advice of her dying mother and behave as a sensible girl would, Bo was, in fact, not sensible at all, and had quite a time of it in the beginning of her quest. That very day she pushed herself up against Peter Peppers, thinking him a fitting candidate, and Peter responded quite favourably, renting out local accommodations for the evening, where they could talk it over. Bo willingly and enthusiastically shed the petals of her flower that night, and slept wonderfully. Peter went home to his family before the sun set, and Bo etched the first of her commandments – no married men.

Well.. at least the married one's wouldn't do as true candidates. But a little practice couldn't hurt, and Bo was pleased with this compromise. As you can imagine, it wasn't long before Bo found herself unwelcome over much of the town.

"What a frustrating position I'm in!" thought poor Bo, and then laughed when she remembered the position she'd been in earlier that day.

Bo plopped down in the long grass, picked petals off petunias, and puzzled out a plan. She'd have to move. Maybe more than once. Her mother had always said 'second best is first worst', and Bo resolved to reach high.

With this in mind, Bo mobilized for a move to the metropolis. All the family belongings were sold, as was their fine little cottage on the outskirts of the village. Money wouldn't be a problem for some time, and the relief and security afforded by funds of this sort allow people to reach for their dreams.

The city was some ways off, and Bo would spend four days in and out of stop over rooms along the way, not once spending the night alone. A butcher, a baker, a candlestick maker, and on the third night she had all three. Rub-a-dub-dub, there was room in the tub, for whom do you think it be? Three lucky men, to find such a hen, that gave it all out for free. They pooled together and left some money on the dresser before going their separate ways, down what tangled paths we are never to hear of again.

Bo considered the money. This was new. She had been given gifts before, but this was the first time she had received money for sex. Bo contemplated the prospects of the two paths before her. If she began accepting money, Bo was sure she could amass a small fortune over a decade and live off the proceeds, independent to the grave. But in her soul Bo did not want to take money for sex. She loved sex! And taking money means you are performing a service, so you'd better perform it well if you want to be successful. She would be competing for those dollars in the trade, and that would sap the joy from her sexuality, a part of herself she loved. Finally, advertising herself as a hooker would forever bar her from changing course and choosing the other path, lest she was willing to start all over again in another town.

A wise woman was her mother, and Betsy would commit to the plan recommended for a girl of her ability and charm. She would daily be depleting her principle funds, but only until such time as she could accomplish an advantageous marriage.

A pure reputation was necessary to bait her fish, so hooking was not acceptable. First, she needed access to the lake where her fish lived.

Bo scouted the richest areas in town over several nights, and charted a course with some good chance of success. Each night a house on any given street lit up like a child given cake, and people would come and go in fine clothes. Bo took note of the women's dress, and had tailored for herself something suitably chaste, yet with the promise of sin. She liked a dress loose below the waist, so she could whet the appetite.

Bo marched confidently, behind a couple, straight up the walkway to a mansion soiree on just one such night.

The butler's head inclined attentively. "I'm Bethany Ann Olivia John. I've been invited by the deputy vice consul for district court 13. I've come with news. Here, take my coat please, thank you. Don't bother, I'll find him myself." A good plan might take some nerve, and Ms. Peep was in no short supply, with the audacity of an airborne aardvark.

First impressions were overwhelming for little Bo Peep. There were men and women everywhere, all of whom seemed easy in their clothes amongst the splendour of wealth. Assaulted on all sides by unimaginable luxuries, try as she might, Bo could not maintain a sophisticated urbane disguise. For five whole minutes Bo wandered like a village booby, in and out of rooms unblinking, her jaw hanging loose, wagging to and fro.

But she soon settled into character, stalking likely prey, and there was none likelier than Phillip von Braun von Winken III, heir to the Winken Blinken spectacles fortune. He was a bit on the young side, but swimming in wealth. Sadly, his parents threw her out that very night. It was a culture shock for little Peep, as fourteen was good and right to marry in her village.

Encouraged by the early success of her new method, Bo boldly barged into yet another evening event, and hooked William Wellersby Woodcock. Billy Bean, Antonio Carlos Alejendras, and Francoise Le France followed. She could hook the fish well enough. The boys were all too eager, one proclaiming love, another marriage, and a third three French hens, among sundry other goods. Reeling one in proved a pickle of pronounced proportions.

It would always go wrong for poor Bo Peep. The first kicked her out on the ride home for expectorating on the floor, apparently another cultural miscue. She thought she was being coy and flirtatious when she flashed the next her panties from the sofa in the living room. He didn't think so, and politely hailed her a ride home, red as a beet. And then she couldn't speak spanish or french, so those relationships never moved in the intended direction. All sorts of wrong directions she had become accustomed to in a previous life were tried.

Poor Bo! But never lose heart! All was not lost. She had learned a valuable lesson. City life was perhaps not best suited to our heroine after all. She might be a Duchess, and yet much disgusted. The life of luxury was a burden to blessed Bo Peep, an upkeep she'd rather not have. She has grown wiser before our very eyes. Bo packed up for a tour of the surrounding countryside, with a new and delightful plan in mind, well on her way to fulfilling the wonders of destiny.

Much to your surprise, yet more petunias were having their petals plucked just around this time. And just whom do you think was plucking the petals off those petunias? This prey is nervous and must me approached delicately, the story teller moving like a cautious doe. We can't charge right at him, we'll frighten him off. He's skittish. Think how horrible, right at this moment, it would be for him to be discovered picking petunias. We chanced upon a glimpse into the very soul of our unsuspecting hero.

Once, one needed his wits in a heartless, competitive world. Survival of the fittest was nature's sharpest tool. But human technological progress has dulled the blade, and now good and all bear children. Those born into wealth need not compete, living atop an ever growing pile of fiat currency. Their good fortune leads to excellent education, and contacts in industries of every sort, well up and away from some hill of financial security that the sweat stained masses scramble to ascend, slipping, inevitably, at the sheerest cliffs.

Some work hard and, while maybe not quite deserve their good fortune, do earn a good portion of it through their own application. Their successes should be congratulated, but should not be attributed to superior ability. Mankind's treasures are buried under a fleshy mass of poverty, undiscovered and forgotten. Work as they might, the outcome is uncertain for the poor. Caution is a mark of intelligence, further hampering the realization of their potential.

Atop the world, gifting out privilege to the already advantaged few, sit the kings on their thrones of gold, and always a place at the table for kith and kin. Such it has been, and such it will always be. Such it was for Robyn Publick, heir to a vast family estate that stretched over vale and valley, gorge and glen, and bog and basin, so vast that a crow might fall out of the sky before he made the length of it.

Robyn, at present picking petunias to present them as a package to his first cousin Princess Penelope Publick, was raised very gently from his crib and placed into a nominal administrative position in government as a favour to the Publick Trust for making vast returns for the state, in some fishy Public-Publick partnership. This gave Robyn ample time to romance among the clouds on one meadow or another about the estate.

Over the crest of the gently rolling hills swaddling the meadow, descended a heavenly figure lifted from a fairie tale, in a light blue frock trimmed with white frilled blouse, bouncing deliciously down the flowers. Robyn was delighted.

"Pardon me sir, but my sheep have wandered off, and I'm in a fix to find them." How she bent and pressed her knees together! "Have I trespassed on your estate? I'm so very sorry for what I've done. I'm completely at your mercy. Only my sheep! Have you seen them?" At this Bo feigned feint, and went to her hands and knees, crawling needy to poor helpless useless Robyn.

"Just lie here a minute, Miss, and calm yourself. You're in such a blush, I can't hear what you're saying." A welcome invitation and Bo cuddled up close, then pushed her face into his thighs. Some say the prophecy was fulfilled that very moment.

"Maybe you should come back with me, Miss, to the Manor House. We can get cleaned up and refreshed before we have a chat about your wool." And they were off, over the valley and across the vale, through the gorge and past the glen, around the bog, and into the basin, where the Manor House sat, whispering wishes conspiratorially along the way.

This marvel of milkmaid handicraft, so slight and light as to flutter on wings, but with the healthy milk capacity of a ravenous dairy cow, so completely enchanted our impressionable Robyn that vows were exchanged on that very walk. "Mother!", he would say, "Mother will adore you. You're her picture of perfection. Mine too! I'll lather you in luxury and affection." Robyn soon spied his mother, inspecting the gardener's work on the hydrangeas, on the left middle of the back beds.

"Is that you Robyn? Who is that you have with you there? Heaven has opened and dropped us an angel."

There was a sudden warmth to the air, a slowing down in time, the setting of concrete around a legacy.

"Little Bo Peep has lost her sheep and doesn't know where to find them!"

"Leave them alone, and they'll come home, wagging their tales behind them."

Robyn, his mother, and Betsy Ann Olivia John Peep withdrew into the converging mysteries of time, space, and vast fortune.

RED RIDING HOOD

Sally was a sassy little minx. She would swish left and swish right as she pierced through a crowd in her trademark red riding hood, intent but graceful. Little Red travelled like light among the market people, unimpeded and unimpeding, but always pleasing. She bargained for her purchases with cunning and deceit. The shopkeep rarely minded. The shopkeep's wife, on the other hand, would chase off Sally with a broom when appropriate. That was every time Red showed up, according to the shopkeep's wife. Red knew all this, and licked her lips as she watched another wife abandon her helpless husband at the stall.

Grandma had taught Sally everything she knew. Grandma was an ace. Grandma made a fortune on the streets in her day. Now she was finely ensconced in the family cottage, out the way a bit. A fine little cottage, surrounded by a fine little fence. Not a picket fence, for she had taste and that would be cliché. Trunks of little trees. Not quite saplings, for that's forbidden. But little more than, with more money than sense. At least the one's she was after. Was I talking about the trees she used for her fence? Right. Good wood. She polished the bark off, sanded them down, and stained them. They made a fine little fence for Grandma around her fine little cottage.

A finely kept carpet of grass decorated her yard. Maybe she'd let it go a little bit, but that happens at her age. And who was she keeping it up for anyhow? That's the way she thought of it. She kept the drapes clean, and those looked great. They still got looks to this day from the admittedly rare passers by. Grandma clearly wasn't quite done with her own sassiness, and could she ever be, really? Some things are innate.

Sally came of an age and Grandma passed on all that she was to Sally, including her lucky red riding hood. Grandma's own mother had worn that riding hood in her time, and Grandma owed much to the cumulative knowledge of family tradition. Sally respected her matrilineal lineage. She cherished her red riding hood, well willing to take up the mantle with all the feistiness and confidence of youth, but often felt imposed upon to live up to a reputation that she didn't yet deserve. The burden of the hood weighed heavy on her heart, but she felt greatness in her soul.

Sally still went to school, on the advice of Grandma. It was a superb social training ground. After working her way through the student hierarchy, all positions, she was finally expelled for supposedly seducing several of the staff, according to their wives. For the time being, Sally slept at Grandma's during the day.

What about her parents you ask? Who knows about her father, she never had one as far as she knew. Her mother sadly passed of a suspicious syphilitic infection gone wrong, septicemia I think. Sally was only seven. Grandma Sybil, on her mother's side, supported Sally since then.

We might as well get introduced to some of the other characters at this point. Will the axe man steps forward. He supplies Grandma with firewood, no charge. Will can be seen at Grandma's cottage from time to time. He's a big, burly teddy bear. Bears look like that, but they have a temper. Like a lot of wild animals, they commit to an encounter absolutely, their attention never waivers. If he's mad, you can bet he means it. Forewarned is forearmed.

And, of course, the new comer to the glens and dales and forests and woods that cover the ravines and valleys and vales and such about and around Grandma's snug little cottage must be met. The light glints off the silver, streaking through his slightly dishevelled but otherwise almost regal mane of thick warm fur. His steps are measured, he is alert, he is a philosopher of sorts. And he has not met his match, or he wouldn't be alive. He is, of course, the wolf.

Wolf had a lot of territory to cover, but he knew every inch of it. And he was the unquestioned, unchallenged monarch of his realm. An aficionado of fine venison, Wolf stalked his elusive prey across great distances and at great expense. He genuinely enjoyed the hunt. But, like many a monarch before, Wolfie's appetite then extended to the abnormal.

Having satiated his every desire, Wolf had somewhat dulled his lust for life. Being a highly intelligent mammal, he considered his prospects carefully. Wolf was fifty seven wolf years old. How many good years did he have left? Any day now some cub, young and hungry, fresh off of privation, lean and taut, could come and de-throne our hero. Wolf wasn't about to let his life pass him by, resting on his laurels. Meanwhile, he understood that the fate of all wolves was sealed and he would be no exception. Something of the carpe diem seized Wolfie, and he began to look about through new eyes.

Wolfie began to frequent the corner of the woods with the long path, worn over decades of slight though reliable use, that finished at the fine little cottage, so nicely kept in his opinion. He didn't need or want the grass completely mown. He liked it this way. He took a liking to Grandma. So when Wolfie was full he would find his way over to Grandma. It wouldn't do to spend more than a few days a month skulking around about the cottage, for many reasons. While he might be full now, he wouldn't be so in a short while. Best keep track of his prey. The cottage did attract some of the choicest doe, and Wolfie liked that. That was a plus. But humans weren't entirely accepting of wolves, and there was a threat, as many of them were about these parts of the woods. He'd seen that axe man more than once. That axe man was no joke. Wolfie had given him a snarl of warning, and out came that axe at a dead sprint. Wolfie was out of there fast.

And that little minx! The one with the red riding hood. Wolfie drooled. He wiped it off with the back of his paw. Words can't describe the feelings Wolfie had for Little Red. He called her that, though he knew she was at least a decade his senior, which enticed him all the more. Grown enough, but Wolfie wasn't intending to spoil this experience with a premature provocation. He had time to enjoy Little Red a little longer, for temptation resisted only sharpens the sensation. Every good wolf knew this, and ours was one of the best. I do say was, as he's sadly no longer with us, in case you were wondering. It's been some time, so I'm comfortable talking about it now.

It was now or never for Grandma. Every day was a day too late to wait. Wolfie was determined to have his way. Time was ripe. Off to Grandma's he would go. But who do you think he ran into while following the path? Little Red Riding Hood, picking flowers, a basket of baked goods set down beside her just as dawn broke. Wolfie was less surprised than you'd think. He'd caught Little Red on this path before at about this time. He'd watched her heading into town in the late afternoons. And sometimes he saw her in the garden, or in the kitchen, or in the forest hereabouts at other times of day. Once he took a peek in the window while she slept. He'd seen Grandma more than that.

"Well, well, Little Miss Red! Fine to see you here. How do you do? Are you off somewhere, or can we lie by the river and let the blades of grass tickle our bare feet?"

"Wolf! I thought you weren't near. But here you are!" The honey in her voice drove Wolfie mad. Her hood hugged fetchingly around her. "It's been some time."

"The present is what matters, Miss." He was overcome at first and blurted out an salacious invitation unbecoming his role, but quickly composed himself for the occasion. Obliging, gentle and tame. "I'm glad to see you safe and well."

"Why thank you, Wolf! Thank the stars you're here! I'm all alone in the woods, and I was feeling quite afraid. Luckily the sun's come up just now. But I'd still appreciate an escort. I'd love to lie in the grass beside the river for a little. Will you accompany me? What a kind offer. Come with me over here." And she reached out for Wolfie's paw.

With his paw resting in her little hand, Wolfie was led a few steps off the path, but just for a moment. Wolfie knew this wasn't right. He savoured her touch, and one day it would be all the sweeter. "On second thought, Miss, you go on and indulge with a little nap near the river by yourself this time. I'm really not in circumstances which allow me to dawdle. Until we meet again, my dear." And Wolfie looked longingly over his shoulder as he turned from Little Red back onto the path he had chosen for himself. Wolf felt some of the pain of a loss, but it was overwhelmed by his sense of self-respect. All the sweeter he said to himself, and then grinned in anticipation. Even more so as he took off at a trot towards another fantasy adventure.

It would take a discerning observer indeed to make sense of Little Red at this moment. The slightest hint of disappointment, perhaps, well disguised? A vindictive, steely, self-determination that flashes by? A shrug and a shake of annoyance and acceptance. Then a shadow of concern. Was something not right about that encounter? Something about that Wolf. He didn't seems quite right. She had seen him, of course, just recently skulking about the cottage. Peeked in her window once, the cheeky prick. And his long looks at Grandma hadn't escaped her attention either. That son of a bitch wouldn't dare! Would he? Better be safe.

Little Red took off in a skip and a scamper through the thicket and thatch of the hairy undergrowth of the forest. Relieved in her belief that Wolfie would trot along at a measured pace, prognosticating his wicked plan, Red raced along the tops of the flowers with ease and grace, far outpacing Wolfie and arriving at the cottage with time enough to spare.

Grandma was informed of Red's flanking maneuver. A smile wriggled across her still handsome face, accompanied by a chirp of laughter. Then a rapid giggle and finally a guffaw. "Grandma, please hurry! Wolf will arrive any moment!" Grandma was persuaded to walk a village over and have tea with another member of the sisterhood, while Red performed a ritual punishment upon our presumptuous canine protagonist. Grandma's fire of inner pride was raging, stoked vigorously by Red's audacity. What a lady in Red she would be! One to shame the rest, herself included. And she pitied the wolf, to some degree. He would deserve what he got. But Grandma had often been thought the villain in her own stories, and could empathize with the Wolf. He was punished for his abhorrent proclivities, appetites of which he has little control. Grandma had often satisfied instinctual urges, even some deemed indecent by others, she had been branded for those proclivities by an enraged and increasingly nasty public. C'est la vie. The sisterhood understood. In the sisterhood she could confide. The trip would do her well. And off she went.

Red dashed from the cottage and clambered up the limbs of the cherished giant oak, just outside Grandma's fetchingly fenced yard. Lost among the limbs above the cottage, Sally spied Wolfie trotting impudently towards her, a dozen breaths off, straight up along the main path that might be used by the milkman, the miller, or the mayor himself.

Sally was not an evil creature. As of yet, Wolfie had been nothing but gracious and polite, providing one wasn't to comdemn Wolfie's perverted pubescent peeping behaviour. She would wait and watch as Wolfie chose to cross further and further beyond the morally dubious into the wilfully damned. But was it right to set bait? Thankfully not a puzzle we urgently must solve in the present predicament, thought Sally in her perch.

Wolfie did indeed skulk up to the side of the cottage, right through the yard, on light feet I will say to his credit. Wolfie wasn't some thumping mindless rock breaker. He was a noble creature. Yet as an apex predator, nothing was to stop him from committing breach of etiquette, or in fact law. The temptation was great, and perhaps none of us have the right to judge Wolfie. Perhaps he, too, might be regretful of his own weakness, a redeeming conciliation you might permit an rehabilitated addict. The fact remains, not having endured the same temptation, might we judge Wolfie fairly? Is it for us to say? An existential question for another time.

Wolfie popped up his front paws to the windowsill at Sally's side of the cottage, and they both had a good view, Wolfie of the interior of the empty abode, and Sally of Wolfie's length and girth. Sally saw as Wolfie's tail twitched and swished. Then all of a sudden Wolfie scampered thrice round the cottage, then thrice round himself right after his own tail in fit of frustration. "Damn mine eyes!" cursed a bulge eyed Wolfie. Exasperated, he made a mad dash right at the front door, and to the surprise of all concerned, burst straight through into Grandma's living room. You should be made aware, for the purposes of posterity, that not one dainty artifact littered about the cottage, on sidetables and sills, not a lamp or a curtain was damaged in any way. The solid oak swung wildly open on heavy iron hinges with a bang, but only the rug slid abrubtly before stopping. Even that felt under control, for Wolfie was indeed an admirable specimen of athlete, not anymore at the peak of his abilities, and yet still impressive and not to be underestimated. Wolfie never gets his due.

Now inside, what might he do? How would this work? Wolfie ruminated a moment. Another plan was evolving from the confused fog in Wolfie's brain. But it never got worked out. While Wolfie was taking a moment to compose his thoughts, he had wandered into the long fantasized bedroom. But his thoughts weren't on the moment. He wasn't enjoying anything as he wondered whether it might be best to bolt straight out that door and never come back. But he had sat down on the corner of the bed in the meantime, when he heard a bright, sing-song "Grandma! Are you there?" ring like a bell from just outside the cottage door. Something happened that never happens. And that's why we have this story. Wolfie panicked.

Wolfie scrambled under the generous down comforter, twice the size it need be, spread gloriously across Grandma's four poster oak frame ancestral magic bed. Each Red had said so to the next, for generations past. "This bed is magical!"

Wolfie cowered. It would have passed instantly. How silly of him? That delicious little red hooded delight? In a moment he could have pounced. But he was entranced by the little red butterfly flitting about the space as he shrunk under the cover.

"Grandma! I see you there under the cover. Your eyes are bulging, my dear, and moist! There, there, don't move. I'll straighten things right up. You just lay right there, Grandma." Sally distracted the Wolf by darting to first one spot, then another, arranging. Sally seemed to visit cabinets, and drawers, and desks, and closets, and all four posts of the bed, all the while Wolfie lay nearly motionless under the covers. "Here, Grandma, let me make you more comfortable."

Now, as to what happened next, I must say I'm as incredulous as the rest of you will be. Like it was the most natural motion in the world, as if Wolfie in the bed really were Grandma, Red lifted the covers and Wolfie with them into a seated position in the bed, with Red behind the mass of cover. "What long ears you have, Grandma!" And with deft contortion, Red slipped ropes prepared from the bed posts and knotted them, in one motion mind you, about both of Wolfie's forelimbs. This one act would foreshadow a glorious career of such maneuvers of expert dexterity for our Heroine, the bearer of a mantle, a long reverenced tradition in life, love, and literature.

Wolfie yelped and writhed ferociously, "What sharp teeth you have, Grandma!", but Red was undismayed and undistracted. Safe at the foot of the bed now, Red concentrated, and astoundingly lassoed one of the wolf's hindlimbs on her very first try. It was cinched to a third post in a thrice, and you bet the fourth followed faithfully. Wolfie was in her hands.

Do you see how fast it all happens? Once he's through the door, it's almost all over for Wolfie in a moral sense. He's in a bad way now. Might he deserve it karmically? Is that the question we're asking? Sure, Wolfie had a past of wolf-ing. He had a bitter fight to the death over this very patch of land he now claimed. And he'd eaten more than his fill. Even as a cub he callously let die his brother, for the sake of a buck that might have gotten away had he not given chase.

And what of intention, you might ask. And you would be right to do so. Wolfie certainly did harbour less than charitable intentions upon his arrival at Grandma's door. But he had done so on dozens of occasions previously as well. On all the others he had done no more than, admittedly all too frequently, trespassing upon a lawn. And are we to condemn intentions? How might we surmise accurately the intensity of those intentions. A passing whim or a manic obsession?

What has Wolfie done? But I know well you are waiting to hear what happens now. What's it all about. A knife is a little messy, but Red relishes the poetic moment. The Wolf tied up so prettily gave Red the time to consider. She made her way into the kitchen and rummaged in the medicine drawer for a scalpel she knew she'd find there, among sutures and such that Grandmas like hers were like to keep. She pulled the poker from the fire on her way back to the bedroom.

"Wolf!" and she gave him a good hard slap across the face, "I wish that would be enough for you to learn this lesson. But I know it's not. I'm going to hurt you and you deserve it. My family is umbillically attached to this land. On this land you must never pass. Grandma and I protect the wood at this outpost. We are born of your own spirit. And look at your here! I'm outraged, you nasty prick. We have looked upon you with a benevolent respect. But our relationship is always to be kept at a distance, lest we beckon you. Today I will scar you as a permanent reminder, and then may you go in peace, with a bit of you left here forever, a piece of you dead for what you have done."

Quick as a slip, that scalpel sliced off Wolfie's pride, leaving him sexless for the rest of his days. The iron poker cauterized a howling Wolfie, and he passed out in agony. Coming to sometime later, slathered in anti-bacterial ointment, expertly bandaged, just outside the fetching fence of the cottage, a very different wolf is born, bemoaning his wretched fate. Stopping to sob occasionally, when completely overcome, our poor wolf slunk gingerly away into the depths of the forest, never to be heard from again.

A saucy Sally pickled Wolf's pepper in an appropriate place, setting it on the shelf with satisfaction. Her inheritance of the red mantle was lighter now, light as a feather, and Red skipped to at the rap on the door.

"Well, Hello!" The axe slipped from Will's hand, instantly under the spell of the sisterhood. In a trance he allowed himself led into the deceptively delicate living room of the fetchingly fenced little cottage, just on the outskirts of their town. And there we must leave them, with respect for Little Miss Red's right to personal privacy, a dignity owed to all in the world of the Fairies.

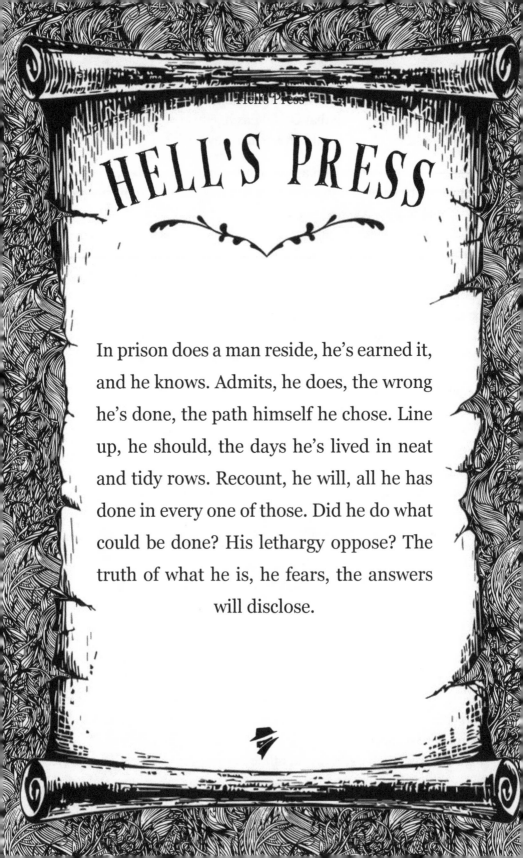

HELL'S PRESS

In prison does a man reside, he's earned it, and he knows. Admits, he does, the wrong he's done, the path himself he chose. Line up, he should, the days he's lived in neat and tidy rows. Recount, he will, all he has done in every one of those. Did he do what could be done? His lethargy oppose? The truth of what he is, he fears, the answers will disclose.

Preface

Shut the door! Don't let them in. They're crowding all around. Crouch down low and hold your breath, beware the slightest sound. Lurking in the bushes and hiding in the trees, eyes are hiding everywhere, these busy little bees. Watch the dance these bees do make, the furor they are in. It's crap, it's trash, it's second rate, It's sacrilege, it's sin. Follow, then, if what you like is what has come before. I feel something deep inside is asking of me more. For those upset, I understand. Please politely use the door.

Open wide the rabbit hole for those that stay inside. A grip upon the edge I have, my foot lodged firm across, arch my back with effort, knuckles dug deep in the moss. Strain I will with all I can, all force must be applied.

In you go, and I behind, down to a realm of mind. What is it that will be inside, what is it that we'll find? More things there are in hell and Earth than dreamt of by our kind. A patient hand is needed for this tangle to unwind.

RUMPELSTILTZKIN

Hark! Ye that have ears to hear, of a time before things had names. Came one of our kind upon the manifestation of evil. Horrorstricken, petrified, he raised a rebelling arm, pointed determinedly at the incarnate evil and yawped "Nuck!"

Evil winced painfully at the name. Fear though he did, our man felt strength. Named then she needn't be so feared. Isolated from all others, Nuck had nowhere to hide. She could not escape the light. She could be seen and called, and her powers were greatly diminished thereby.

Nuck was furious. The man must suffer. She had him bound to a post in a clearing in a valley within the vale. There he remained, fixed to his post, where he suffered the darkest despair. The man strained to maintain his mental balance. But time is merciless, and he would lapse into episodes of psychotic violence, shaking and rattling his post in his agony. Thus evil came to know the man.

Nuck's face contorted into her wicked smile, she raised a bony finger and proclaimed "Rumpelstiltzkin!" and his name was written in the book of the damned by evil herself. All hope was lost. Slowly, but inevitably, he was stripped bare of all vestiges of goodness and virtue. He felt a cold greed take possession of his soul. Nuck had infected him with an insatiable thirst for wealth. Avarice was evil's most terrible curse.

Rumpelstiltzkin would wander the earth, poisoned with a rapacious appetite, taking what he could even from those least able to afford the loss, spreading misery and woe throughout our kind. This is the price he pays for knowing evil.

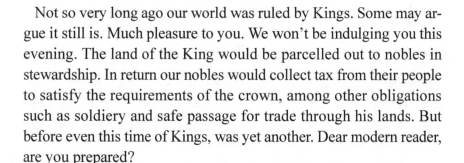

Not so very long ago our world was ruled by Kings. Some may argue it still is. Much pleasure to you. We won't be indulging you this evening. The land of the King would be parcelled out to nobles in stewardship. In return our nobles would collect tax from their people to satisfy the requirements of the crown, among other obligations such as soldiery and safe passage for trade through his lands. But before even this time of Kings, was yet another. Dear modern reader, are you prepared?

The strong were both feared and admired, for they were strong. The village relied for protection upon the strength of the few. One village was indeed very strong for the strength of one man alone. Wigana, was his name. Loud Wigana he was called. He compelled obedience from his neighbours, and with the tribute paid him, afforded an army of some considerable number.

Tribute is taxation. Tribute is theft. Both are true. Security and administration under compulsion is an end to freedom. She did not die with a whisper. Wigana ruled with strength, murdering those who oppose, and collecting his due. Loud Wigana.

One man is the tip of a spear. But he must relegate authority to administer his law. This he did, entrusting the custody of rule over a generous, though bandit plagued and corrupt eastern province, rife with dissent and disorder, to an ally. Freedom would die at the hands of Ikarl for these troublesome independent lands.

In turn Ikarl pillaged the peoples of the east, suffocating them down to the merest subsistence, at the mercy of his tyranny. While Wigana waited patiently, Ikarl refused to offer even partial plunder, claiming the expense of his ever growing force required his entire purse. Ikarl profited handsomely, and was proclaimed locally as King of the East.

The King in his cart sits mountains apart from the masses he tramples beneath. His courtiers and guards, his ministers and bards, graciously baring their teeth. What the King may desire, his soldiers acquire, so the King may most generously unsheathe. Once he is done what he has just begun, the King feels a glorious relief.

A lawless land requires a vigilant and threatening oversight. Thus Ikarl would personally oversee much trade within his purview. Our ruthless tyrant prototype was at this very moment considering the prospects of a Miller, sat squat at the intersection of several villages in the land. All grain for many leagues around brought their stores to be milled by this man. Yet he lived in but a modest comfort. Avarice and ambition are sternly suspicious of innocence and permissiveness.

Walked he, Ikarl, this day to the step before the miller's shop, yet stopped short at the sight in the slanting of light of a pulse of a bright brilliant beauty. This golden shine, he thought, must be mine. With a lustful grin veiled thin to begin let us enter the plot of our tale.

"Good King Ikarl! As a child I played along the riverside with your mother's sister's husband's cousin, Dieter. And here we are together! Of all the hundreds of people I've ever seen in my life, here you are! Who would believe it?"

"Miller, you've done well for yourself I see."

"On this grain business I lose money most of the time. The small farmers, you see, they can't afford my share or they will starve through the winter. I forgo their fees so often that most of the time the mill is turning at a loss. But I have a secret that helps me muddle by. My daughter, a very special girl you see, can spin straw into gold. And so we get by. Hehehe.." Our affable miller was clearly nervous, but chanced familiarity to rescue him from Nuck's malevolence to strangers.

"Miller, I am a direct man. Where is my share of the proceeds of your trade? I will take them now and go, leaving my grace and protection to your family."

"As I told you, dear, King, I have only enough to eat for myself and my daughter. Please!"

"Call your daughter, miller."

The sweating miller cracked falsetto as he dared not pause, and called to his daughter, "Ludmila!"

Slowly out from a creaking door on the second floor stept our sweet young victim, innocence, grace and charm to the slaughter. Down the stair came she swift and fair, with the freedom of air, to be so suddenly ensnared by a captor. Ikarl seized the stunned belle by her wrist and, though she did resist, he would persist, and mounted her behind him on his horse. The miller was hoarse, dazed and displaced, upset and confused, left badly abused by Ikarl the King of the land.

Pricked off at a terrific pace, the pair proceeded upon the path to the Palace. The miller's daughter was not an unwelcome burden, far from it. Ikarl enjoyed immensely the rhythmic prance of his filly, sometimes slowing her down to an oh so gentle, maddeningly measured hip sway, then prick the spurs into a dancing trot, the girl pressed close for comfort and profit. All pretty things know men.

Into the Palace courtyard they rode and Ludmila was dragged once again, for Ikarl was appreciative but not forgiving, up and around the spiral stair tower to a room with a store of straw. Mound upon mound spread thick on the ground, Ludmila looks down to evade the King's frown. "Spin gold from that bed, and I'll give you some bread." the King said, and in they did bring a stool and a sound spinning wheel.

The door shut once and firmly. Ludmila collapsed into the hay, resigned to her helpless fate. Is there no one that cares about Ludmila? Her senseless capture at the hands of a budding tyrant? This impossible injustice? The miller cares. But he can do nothing. The strong will enforce their law. Nuck cares. Nuck took pleasure in the shadows of misfortune she casts across life.

A pulse shivers the shadows suddenly, beyond a corner in the room. Manifest before her becomes the queerest creature ever seen. He was shrivelled and hunched, gaunt and pale, sly and anxious, mischievous but merry, merry but unstably so. His hood pulled back revealing wisps of tonsure, a spare hair tiara about this fallen Prince that dared to name Nuck. High sharp cheekbones sat beside his sunken blacken eyes, decorated beneath by a protruding hook nose, bending to touch its mirrored counterpart, the chin. All was moulded into a deathly complexion of clay, all clothed in a husk of sack and rope.

"Look at the sad girl make water! A man's mouth may lose him a daughter. Your fortunes are dire, my dear. I have a proposition for you to hear. Would you like to live long, a life filled with song, and riches and health and never cause to fear?"

"Oh, yes, sir! Whatever will I do? This straw must be spun into gold or the King pulls off my pretty head. I'm at your mercy, sir!"

"Then I am your saviour. I will this very night spin the straw to gold. In return you will part with that alluring necklace you hold."

"My mother's pearls? She's dead you know. That's Nuck."

"The pearls or you die!" an enraged eruption from a hopping red elf man heated the room.

Ludmila fingered the pearls of her ancestral heirloom. "I agree."

The little man clapped his hands and cackled with brilliant delight. He hopped onto the stool before the spinning wheel and began to feed it the straw hand over hand while pumping vigorously at the pedal, and out the other side strands of gold began to pile at their feet. Faster and faster worked the goblin man while the gold thread gathered. He continued to work feverishly until the moon reached its zenith, and the last of the straw had been spun.

Wiping the sweat from his brow, the imp hopped off the stool, strafed back and forth in front of the sleeping Ludmila, finally snatching at the pearl necklace, tearing it from her neck, and vanishing into the darkness of his corner.

Ludmila awoke in awe of the heaps of gold thread, but inconsolable for the grief of her loss. The King came. Unable to restrain the acquisitive impulse, he had some guards place our poor Ludmila into an even larger larder loaded yet more heavily with stores of straw. He called through the closing door, "Spin this straw and I will most certainly spare your life and that of your thieving father, my dear."

Within a moment of finding herself alone once again, Ludmila skipped, in a game of corners, about the room calling out.

"Elf man! Elf man! Where are you hiding? Great goblin relieve me of suffering and woe! I have but one treasure to offer your honour, my most cherished token, may it be worthy of your favours. This ring on my finger was a gift from Wigana, who swore it once graced a bishop in Rome. Please take this in trade for the spinning of wonders and free this poor bird to go home!"

The shadows shivered opposite our girl, forming into our avaricious imp, hopping bow legged, foot to foot with wonderful speed and agility, cackling merrily all the while.

"I'll spin the whole lot for that bishop's rot and free this sparrow from harm. Lie down now, tot, and let not in your thoughts of troubles and worries alarm. Your saviour I'll be once again, and then in the end we'll settle our fee."

An glowing yellow dawn spread lustre about the golden room as Ludmila awoke to wonder yet surpassed. Towers of gold thread bound about in every corner. The bishop's ring has vanished, and the door to her turret cell opens to reveal King Ikarl of the East. Elated at the immensity of fortune's favours, he once more locks our Princess in yet another warehouse, stacked with straw for the stables, here for winter storage.

"My dear, my darling, my love, my queen! What a strange and tangled torture our love has been. Such wonders as yours the world has never yet seen. Once more, my dear, my darling, we'll marry next day! Once more, I beg you, to an empire your love paves the way!"

Alone before the impossible once again, Ludmila had nought to do but call for fortune's favour, in a growing fever of anxious torment. Appeared from the fog of the darkness and shadow evil's most awful disease, an appetite voracious, unsleeping, unfettered, infecting the world at Nuck's ease.

"I've nothing to offer! Oh what shall I do? My great goblin saviour, please have pity and ask of me what I can afford. I am desperate and at your mercy, my lord!"

Bent, now, to hands and knees is the tortured wicked soul of man, so hollowed with greed that it serves as his only satisfaction. The face of evil sits still, staring intently into the eyes of our poor impoverished princess, as he decides what to take.

"I will spin this straw to gold in one single night, while you sleep, dear girl. You will be saved, you will marry this King and you will become Queen. In time you will bear him a child. This child you owe to me. I will return soon after the birth to conclude our agreement. You are saved, princess, and you will live long and in comfort. Now sleep."

Under threat of death what will man not sacrifice? Must we stand stalwart, shoulder to shoulder with our principles and virtues at death's most pressing advance? And if we are permitted moral flexibility in times of mortal crises, then how far will this benevolent laxity allow us to slide? If the risk is great to one's survival, some amount of self interest at perhaps minor cost to others can be argued legitimate. An worthy discussion, an web of irreducible complexity, an conundrum. Go and seek an answer so you can begin to be what you now consider yourself.

Ludmila slept soundly and well, waking to a hark and a knock on the door. The king, in three steps, came to his knees, hands clasped, preserving what dignity and composure he could as he fell weeping in joy to the cold stone floor of the storeroom. Ludmila became wife to King Ikarl and Queen in the East that very day.

Won't the animals go hungry now that their feed has become gold? Good Queen Luddy saw to the purchase of grain and straw and sundry other goods from all the land. Merchants, farmers, artisans, and tradesmen of all sorts wore heavy pockets on their pants. Having only converted a modest fraction of their gold to coin and sending it out amongst the towns and villages of the province, Ludmila had invigorated the land. Queen Luddy embraced change. She sought engineering solutions to all the questions her people might face. Fertilization and land management increased yields. Water flows were successfully diverted, permanent reservoirs created, and fish catch counted and measured. Jurisprudence was forced to wield a pen that would restrain the sword. Ikarl's security force established an more formal working bureaucracy with restrictions and safeguards to protect the people, and regular patrol of public ways to ensure safe passage for goods and persons throughout the land. Despite the burden of taxation, the people and their rulers prospered.

An abundance was created. In the autumn harvest of her third year as Queen of the East, Ludmila bore child. Throughout her term she oscillated between anxious and frantic, worrying the palace physician into peevish prognostications. Days passed after the birth and the Queen's dementia improved, but was replaced by an suffocating depression. Moons swung on a rope round about the earth, as the earth did about the sun, and the child loved by misery grew bathed in tears.

In late summer of the child's first year, a fierce heat flooded the land from the west, burning the crops before harvest had begun. From murders of scavenging blackbirds, to swarms of locusts that blot out the sun, and a rain of frogs falling splat from the sky after a thunderous storm, ill omen beset King Ikarl into autumn.

Night fell early on the tenth day of the tenth month as a blanket of black cloud covered the earth in shadow. Candles walked wearily through the dark silence of the sweating palace walls. One such light was lifted by the hand of the Queen herself, shook from her sleep by a clap of thunder, and stirred by faint whispers from the thick of the dark. Always and ever but steps just ahead of her, Luddy was lured with a snap. Through rooms and through halls, she heeds evil's call to spring her malevolent trap.

Opening now the heavy door of the storeroom, the vanishing light of her candle blew through the stores of hay and illuminated the elf man, head bowed, seated on a stool before the miller's daughter once again.

"I have come for the child."

"You mustn't!" The Queen pleaded.

A sudden rage erupted from the dwarf, as his face boiled, he leapt clear his height and plunged violently into the stones, cracking one considerably with the stomp of his tiny foot.

"The child is mine, you slithering slime! I'll curse your whole family disease! Famine and drought, hobbled with gout, you'll scrape and you'll beg on your knees! You're nothing! You're crap! You're wretched and foul! And I will enslave your miserable soul!"

"Great Goblin grant me one last gasp of hope before you drown me in the ocean of despair! I beg of you, for anything that I have to give, it is yours! I have riches beyond counting. Gems the size of a child's foot. Ancient and powerful amulets, rings and bracelets. I can satisfy your heed, your greed, your every need, but let my child alone!"

"My patience stretches thin! Your treasures now are worthless tin. The child I'll take and make it mine, ere love will conquer Nuck in time. I'll cast aside the chains and purse, and lift from under evil's curse. We made a bargain, you and I, And you will honour thy word!"

"I will not break my oath. Find favour in your cruelty, and do with me what you will, but grant me this last flicker of time!"

"In the dark of night, when the raven takes flight from your window sill, Princess, you'll come. With child in your arms, no tricks or cheap charms, you will hand the child over to me. Defy me once more and me dear I assure you my mercy will not match my wrath. "

The elf evaporated into the shadowed walls, the echo of his evil heartbeat started a stuttered reverberation rippling through the castle stones. That night Ludmila, Queen of the East, clutched close to her child, weeping the child to worry. Morning came and the Queen would not part from the girl. Worry progressed to hysteria, and the child suffered. The Queen allowed the child to be taken from her and, in a tense fever, the Queen went on a walk through the tangled paths of the woods as the sun receded beyond the rolling hills.

The night forest suffocates the Queen in darkness, yet her steps are quick, with a nervous anxiety. Would she know were the wither and where of her wanderings whispered to her from whence the fates weave their wonders? Through the growth guarding a path the Queen pushes, passing into a glade by a stream. A hill by the stream has been seen in a dream. An homely hovel has been shovelled quite snugly just there. From the far side of the home spies the Queen a small fire. And then the small elf man unplugging a jug!

A stumble, a hop, a skip and a shake, the goblin stomps madly, the ground beneath quakes. "Tonight, tonight my plans I make. Tomorrow, tomorrow the baby I take. The Queen, she blunders away this game, for she knows not the power to claim by the forcing out of evil's name!"

The goblin hopped about the fire, stewed in jug liquor, crouching and rubbing his palms together, then erupting into wild eyed fervor, and shooting another swig of his goblin juice to compliment his dance.

"I'll have her guess, I'll give her three. A little hope, I'll say, you'll see. If she can guess, she's won the game. How could she win? For Rumpelstiltzkin is my name!"

Queen Ludmila made her escape in quiet haste, back through the tangled paths of fate, to the keep of her castle, where she slept soundly with her child, the raven loitering here and there a top the windowsill. The day following, Ludmila held close to the child through her meals until the moon pushed the sun out of the sky once again, a third since evil's hand had come to claim her. As the castle settled in slumber, clouds covered the land, blocking out the eyes of the heavens. Evil moves amongst the shadows, and, at a flash of lightening, the raven leapt from the windowsill into the starless night sky.

Queen Ludmila, carrying the child, shuffled through the halls towards the storeroom, tense with uncertainty, but certain advantage she owned. Opening now the heavy door, greeted by evil's sour breath, Ludmila paused. Evil's noxious emission bled into the hall. Ludmila, nerved in myelin steel, pushed into the smog of Nuck with the child in her arms.

"Have you now the child in arms, ready to submit? Pass her here, our deal is done, as is right and fit."

"Goblin, no! You mustn't? The child is innocent and true. In her lies hope, the last we have. I'm yours! Take me. You I will obey. Leave the child, your slave I'll be this day."

The elf begins to vibrate, ever faster, with ever more fury, a glowing about him, the room begins to heat. Then his vibration settles, and a wide squinted merry twinkling murderous smile opens lips to sharpened teeth and wormy tongue. A slow staccato cack crackles. Lips press, cheeks puff, switch flick, and the elf booms in maddened joy.

"Guess my name, you tyrant's whore! Guess my name! The child is yours. Guess my name! We'll meet no more!"

And with his proposal, a strung was plucked on the web of fate. Ludmila, the miller's daughter, Queen of the East and her tormentor, a soul twisted by the curse of Nuck, succumbed to the wave and harmonized to the key of destiny. The Queen did not quail, as the goblin had expected. Was that a curl at the corner of her lip? "I think it begins with an R, elf man, I can feel it in my bones!"

The goblin gasped and bared his upper incisors, looking the ass. "Not a Rikalus or a Ramsboord. Or an Regan or Repine. A Rass, a Rammer, Rhone, Remasque, a Rouge or an Raquorqet. You evil rogue, I know you and I'll beat you at your game. For I have hold upon your soul, a power I will claim, as I isolate the evil - Rumpelstiltzkin is your name!"

See the goblin shake! A tension builds in every nerve and fibre in his face. He pushes blood into his skull, and the vibration begins, first in the head, soon the core and limbs, he's reddening, maddening, soon to explode. He arches his shoulder blades, baring his chest, throwing his head back, roaring to the heavens an primordial syllable of defeat, plucking a string on the web yet again. The goblin launches thrice his height from the floor, plummets impossibly, like a bolt of darkened lightening, plunging his left leg to the hip into the stone floor with a mighty boom. Roaring in rage, the elf plants his right leg on the floor between two prepared arms, pushes with an furious evil, tearing the left from his hip with a thunderous roar, waking the gods and anointing the tale of Rumpelstiltzkin to the pantheon legend of lore.

The candle settled to steady flicker, as candles do. Mother turned to her child, smiled, took her hand, and led her on to the dark paths of forever forgotten, forever more.

GOLDILOCKS

Of all the advantages that are bestowed upon a child, none are as insidious as beauty. The ugly child earns his social pleasures through trial and toil. His failures only enhance the sensation of success. The beautiful child is the loved child. First impressions are lasting, and as the world smiles at the child, the child smiles back.

Moral true North is never properly established for the beautiful, for their trespasses are less aggrieving. For ugly, the path of moral integrity is frighteningly narrow, dropping steeply to abyss on either side. Pretty can roller skate drunk and blindfolded in a kindergarten, yet still be considered acceptably moral. Ugly will be okay. It's just a broken ankle. How stupid of him to be in the way.

Pretty has a different name in each story there is to tell, and in this one her name happens to be Tiffany Isabella Tatiana Sinclear. The boys she spurned and the girls, sweating green envy, thought of a clever nickname for her, I wonder can you guess? Her being a mouthful, she was commonly referred to by her long luxurious hair, as Goldilocks. Hi Goldie. Everyone is so happy to meet you, you lucky girl.

Parenting was strange and foreign to the Sinclears. A baby for 5 minutes is an ice cream like treat. A baby for 5 years is intolerable. The child's basic needs were met, she was paraded triumphantly among guests, but when the bright lights dimmed and the spectators withdrew, Tiffany was to be tucked away in a cupboard like a kettle. Goldie grew up feral. Food was on the table at regular hours, but Goldie came and went as she pleased, sometimes pausing her self serving escapades just long enough to wring some silver out of the fleeting spectres that passed as her mother and father.

"But I want it! You will give it me!"

And give it they would, caring more for tonight's fish than their selfish daughter. Everything would turn out just fine for her, for she has been kissed by the angel of fortune. Which is true. With everyone so willing to help, how could she but succeed.

I must apologize. I have been very unkind to our young heroine. I get carried away, for I am prejudiced against her. What has she done to deserve the slander I have heaped upon her? I haven't supported my claims thus far, and I shouldn't paint fair Goldilocks entirely in black. Though selfish by nature, she could work well with others, provided they did what she said. She liked to shine, and worked for praise when it suited her to do so. Impetuous, indeed, impertinent on occasion, but well mannered when being so was important, and often enthusiastic in her doings. There, there, Goldie. You're a sweet girl. What a charming pout!

All this to sow the seeds of doubt in the reader's mind. What is Goldilocks? How are we to stand in judgment of this misguided tale? Is she a poor neglected child, understandably finding her way into trouble? Is she sweet and saintly, as she would have you believe, and in her innocence she has mounted a sacred cow, lucky to escape with her honour and her life? Is she a menace? Should she be shackled and beat?

Goldie was blissfully unaware of the perils that preyed along her very path, and the import they would have as an eternal echo. As far as she was concerned any and all paths were for her choosing, and she may walk where she pleased. Applaud as she goes if you agree, for the sake of proper appearances, appearances befitting a fabled princess.

And go she did one early morn, humming a lullaby, along one of these paths into the fog of a vast forest, said to be peopled by genies and sprites and fairies of all sorts. Handy excuses are in ready supply for the husband that arrives home late and dishevelled. It's the truth, too, if you squint.

What was she to find in the depths of that darkened forest? Love, romance and passion? Sage soulful wisdom? Innocence to experience? An ascension into a pantheon of legends?

Forests begin abruptly, and within a song one can become completely lost. Goldie would sometimes become lost in a grocer's, so we'll forgive her for not recounting exactly where she went. Does that mean that she is useless as an witness to her life? Far from it. Her recollection is in experience, encounters, emotions and impressions, and she was a trouve of useful material.

As the lullaby concluded, the thick quiet of the forest engulfed our heroine. Goldie felt herself naked a moment, and submissively allowed the dictates of destiny to direct her.

A cricket jumped up and danced on her shoe. He bid her a gracious 'miss, how do you do?' With a bow and a scrape, he hopped clear once again, letting Goldie's excursion ensue.

She'd been this way and that, and one stone looked much like another. An adventure turned fretful, Goldie knew not where she was, nor where she might be going. Trying to keep all the trees on a line on her right, losing her line, and then trying all the ones on the left, hopelessly entangled in a web she weaves herself, until finally Miss Goldie happens upon a queer little cottage set apart in the bush.

"What a queer little cottage," exclaims Goldie to herself. "I'll go in, have a look."

Was the door open? It was unlocked, yes, over the threshold, and she's in. In a kitchen. With a table, as one might expect. But not a table like this. Three frightening bear legs held a carved table top, inset with bear teeth. There was a reddish stain to the wood in many places, making a horrific macabre impression on sensitive Goldie, who suffered a shiver of piano key scales to run up and down her spine, collapsing her in the nearest chair.

The chair was also carved she noticed. Carved with delicate care. Carved with the inspiration of the gods. And on a place mat in front of dear Goldie lay a porcelain portion of apparently pumpkin soup. Could be carrot, thought Goldie. A few handsome sprigs of parsley garnished with appeal. Three settings. Goldie picked up the spoon.

With effort, as the spoon was cast iron. "Cold," thought Goldie and spied a bowl beside, steam rising, the spoon a finely hammered silver. "Ha, Hot!". One more try, and it's just right. She gobbled up the bowl without a thought, a delicious pumpkin, and Goldie throws up a fist of achievement.

Time for a snoop. Goldilocks rummages about, in a delicate, girl-ish way, not the rampaging male buffoon, but the deft ascertion of all secrets, and the room remained, to all inspection, untouched.

The immediate fear of her situation had well subsided since the soup. The snoop was a thrill, and she threw herself into a chair with a crack. "Aach!" The ache in her back! The chair was as hard as a rock. It was, indeed, a rock, cunningly carved and stained to a wood. "Poof!" she sunk into a cloud, suffocating the struggling girl. "Ah," sighed Goldie on the third chair, "just right." Goldie pumps a fist of success, and the unfortunate chair, as fine as it might be, collapses under the slight celebration of Miss Gold.

After sometime ruminating in her narrow mind, Miss Goldilocks, burn her at the stake, decides she is falling in love with this third bear. Sharing sensibilities much to her liking, she had a burning desire to know more about this pauper prince charming, in the woods, a master artist, undiscovered and pure. She scampered up the steps. Into the bedroom.

Once again there were three. Cautious and knowing, Goldie drags the pads of her fine white fingers over the first, stony dark bed. And again over the pure fur of the second. Goldie lay atop the final bed, rolling with a close eyed smile, under the covers until she was curled right up in her lover's cocoon. And soon was sound aslumber.

The door opens, sometime later, and home come the family. The soup marks a surprise. The chair an outrage, it took weeks to carve. Villain! And the worst was yet to come. But come it does, and now. The Bears find a woman, a child, a doll, sleeping soundly in the third bed.

Papa Bear races, enraged, to the encroacher, latching on to her with his powerful hands. The others are a flutter of limbs in a chaos, as screeching Goldie progresses to beseeching martyr on her way to the door. To the door there's a roar! And another fierce roar, and a savage and scathing abuse as Goldie is tossed on the floor. Papa pushes Goldie out, and shakes fate with the slam and a final roar behind the closing of this tale's door.

HELL'S PRESS

In prison does a man reside, a punishment for birth. Suffer, will he, while he's here, to fate's eternal mirth. He may well wonder, time to time, what life is really worth. Why must he wander, lonely, to his grave beneath the earth. But never while he's curled up, cozy, on a rug beside the hearth.

Preface

Affection is not out of place in this world. Abundant is love. We need time to unfurl a tapestry of woven fabric, fine in every way. A world in which one wanders, wonders, not alone.

Live in the valleys and vales of beyond, three little piggies , their whiskers still blond. Their mother, she dotes on them, has since their birth. But now she must yield to the turn of the earth. Piggies grow bigger as seasons roll by, and time comes when piggies from mother will fly in haste to a future they've dreamed of before, with grandiose mansions and butlers by doors.

Scheming and planning for future to come, to danger and risk our piggies grow numb. Who is that lurking about in the wood? I needn't tell you, yet I think I best should. He's gracious, you see now, in all the right ways, he's cunning and guileful and tricky and sleek, deceitful , deceptive, he preys on the meek. Tenacious, I vow, you shan't meet his gaze. His name is synonymous with none other than Nuck. But I needn't tell you.

You've had the good fortune.

THE THREE LITTLE PIGS

Let not this gruesome tale advise the reader to paint all creatures of a species with the same brush.

I, myself, once experienced a failing of this sort. I came upon a man so much like myself that I was stunned, and could not tell us apart, even under threat of death. My doppelganger, however, was suffering some emotional distress, as his face was contorted in anger, flushed red, with angry black squinted slits burning hateful, hidden eyeballs. It dawned upon me then that though we may be similar in countless ways, yet one should be careful mistaking between the two.

To my great surprise, at that very moment I became aware that, indeed, I was regarding myself, in a giant mirror where one was not expected. And I had a new revelation – that maybe characteristics are shared identically between us all, only varying in degrees. I've often thought so as I observed an insect closely and quickly understood his purpose, cheering him on in his task. And sometimes I've thought so as I reflect upon the fate of the pigs and the wolf in this very story.

A pig is much more easily understood than an insect, owing to our similarities. Shelter and food, the need to feel loved, pigs share a great deal with the majority of mankind. Wolves, on the other hand, can only be understood by a select few. If you find yourself worried that you don't properly understand the nature of the wolf and cannot empathize with his predicament, I will do my utmost to show Wolfie in his best possible light, so as to alleviate your burden. Though that may prove difficult in this instance, as Wolf does little to recommend himself favourably. He's out to slaughter fat tasty pigs, after all.

Wolf had a long and noble reign as unquestioned monarch of the forests and dales and glens and ferns of the upper valley, even extending a goodly ways into the mountain terrain beyond. For nine long, generally peaceful, years the valley was protected from fearsome predators by our hero, that silver backed gentlemen meandering along. He clearly hasn't seen want for some time. What bravado! What style! What easy confidence, as he weaves an independent path across the land.

Unthreatened, Wolfie had the leisure to philosophize. With nothing to get terribly excited about day after day, Wolfie felt he had lost a little of the lust for life characteristic of his younger years. Sniffing out a doe hardly perked his ears for some time past. Now as the sun begins to set on his glorious career, Wolfie unfortunately let fall the rope.

What rope you might well ask. You should. Those of you pretending you know to which rope I am referring without me saying so directly are entertaining conjecture unworthy of the scholar. Enjoyable as it may be, one must remain disciplined and not jump to outrageous conclusions, even if you have unearthed evidence that well supports your claim.

For those of us not pretending to the scholarly, we can immerse ourselves in the world of interpretation, and approach the work free of all pretension, free to squeeze every last ounce of joy from the pages we clutch.

What rope, you might ask. The one we all hold in our hands. The tendency to ignore moral norms and pursue our pleasure down ethically dubious paths. The rope could be a leash, if you like, holding back an inner demon. Maybe it's not a rope after all, or any sort of thing like that. It's the real you being restrained, and the moral norms are a cage in which you are trapped. Maybe it's a ladder we climb towards moral purity, sliding down and breaking steps along the way in our ethical blunders.

Wolfie let go of a rope like that. His appetites began to stray into the abnormal. His perversions would worsen greatly in time, but for now he happened to have an unnatural taste for those three fat piggies growing handsomely on the outskirts of the village. At the appropriate age, these three were ready to set out on their own, leaving the warmth and safety of their childhood home to lay claim to some small portion of the world. Something they could call their own. Some stake they would plant, and maybe run up a little flag, announcing to the world that, yes, they were here and they mattered.

Dreams of a fat little piggy wife were indulged by all three. Her bending, tending the pot draped over the coals, little piglets running about, maybe one of the uncles playing a tune. A field of crops grows through the season, expertly managed by the shrewd hand of piggy, farmer savant.

Not one of them so much as glanced back at mother as her tears dropped on the lawn and she sadly waved a feckless trotter. She even fell to the ground in emotional collapse before they were out of sight. The ungrateful beggars couldn't give a tinkers toss. Such are the ways of youth. Not that these would have time to regret it.

Mother was overreacting, as usual. How far could a newly adult piggy get? They had already told her of the land that they had found, somewhat deeper into the forest, opening into a vast clearing, with a fresh vigorous stream running through, on which their hopes and dreams relied. With three of them keeping up filial appearances, her home would rarely be empty after all. Though it was, in fact, as only one piggy went home once in the following six month. It was pig Two. He didn't think he'd need a towel. But now he thought he'd rather have one, so he was going back to ask mother.

These three helpless little piglets did not yet comprehend the nature of the world, and strode confidently into the jaws of jeopardy. Our wolf may be slightly more rotund than you'd expect. But don't let that deceive you. Wolf was as wily as they come, and was yet to be out manoeuvred on his own terrain. Wolfie knew what was happening with those piggies, and recently he woke from a wet dream, even at his age, about that bacon.

Wolfie stalked out that clearing well, and in his addictively competitive way, wore out dozens of forest paths snaking through the surroundings, in preparation. He would mutter to himself, rehearsing interactions, agreeing, disagreeing, pleading, persuading, became irate with himself once or twice, and bumped into a tree, huffing eureka, nearly falling in the stream when finding the right words to complete his ditty:

Piggy, little piggy, let me come in! No?! Then I'll huff, and I'll puff, and I'll blow your house in!

Wolfie would tumble around in ecstatic laughter, wild eyes bulging and wet, then shut tightly in unendurable hilarity, gasping for breath.

Wolfie, having arranged his network of forest paths to his liking, moved off from the clearing he had named Piggy Trap, giving space and time for these three young oinkers to establish themselves on this ripe piece of real estate. Surely these piggies weren't so stupid as to not notice the smell of wolf in the vicinity. But, given time, they would be lulled into feeling secure. Wolf would let that time ripen further. In the fall, he would return to a triumphant and glorious feast on these three arrogant hams. Wolfie was off at a trot into the shadows of sunset.

I realize you don't know our piggies all that well at this point. Nor am I going to dive into the details of their upbringing, or their childhood experiences. That may be well and good, that you would clamour for some snippet or anecdote telling you more about each of the piggies, in your insatiable greed, your lust, your passion to know all. All you need know of the piggies will be told in this one character revealing tale.

Curious that despite all their other markings of civilization, like their adorable green patterned lederhosen, or their slightly German accent when they spoke English, their native language by the way, these pigs didn't actually have proper names, as you would well expect. They were simply called piggy number One, piggy number Two, and piggy number Three. They were the surviving three of a litter of thirteen, all these many years later. Best not to dwell on the fates of the others too much. Yes, some are interesting, and maybe more, one is extraordinary after all. But piggies One, Two, and Three are the focus of our tale.

They had received equivalent educations, were loved equally by their parents, shared equally in chores and community activities, and yet, as you will see, how very different could be the inclinations of these three little porkers. When, many years later, mother came to know of the doings and happenings of her little piglets, she was overcome with conflicting emotions, tearing her in one direction and the next. She suffered a psychotic collapse, and was rushed to hospital. She lived on another 26 months or so, but only as a shell of her former vivacious piggy self. She was listless and distracted, never quite recovering from the shock, and slowly slipped into the sorrow of eternal slumber.

On with the doings. Piggy number One was a slovenly disgrace of a pig. His mother would have been humiliated had she seen the filthy, dissolute life lived by her own loved little chopper. From day one in Piggy Glen, number One lazily propped a half bale of hay, tepee style, around the trunk of a fair sized deciduous in one corner of the clearing, and proceeded to lay about in the sun all day, rolling in the muck for some protection against the searing mid day heat. Never once did he deign to shuffle through the stream, even at the intimidating behest of his slightly more civil brothers.

Once the field work was undertaken, it must be said, piggy number One did his fair share and not without good humour. Some say piggy number One is the true philosopher of the bunch. Socrates would have approved, for piggy number One loved the company of all the living creatures of the valley, and would try to mate with any he could. His unrelentingly cheery demeanour softened the woes from all his failings and troubles. He contributed his fair share of the work, and he would thereby share in the spoils. How he arranged his finances was none of anyone's business. He was accused of, and in fact quite guilty of, low, some would say unacceptable, moral conduct on more than one occasion, once even meriting the attention of the local constabulary, whom duly made call at piggy number One's former residence and frightened his mother out of her wits for a day, until someone from the department called to reassure her that the peeping case had been put on the back burner as no one, herself included, quite knew where piggy number One was at.

Piggy number Two might look positively industrious next to his slothful brother number One, but I wouldn't give him a pass for his own adolescent delinquencies. Once again, none could fault this piggy for his field work. All participated and all were handsomely rewarded. Whatever number One did with his income, no one could tell. He didn't seem attracted to wealth or luxury. His clothes could've been a tinkers second choice. Some secretly believe number One had amassed a fortune, and the treasure has never been re-covered. Whole hobbyist clubs have been found out in pursuit round these parts. Whatever piggy number One had hidden in his closet, number Two was the opposite. He was an extrovert, and every bless-ed soul in the valley knew where his money went.

Piggy number Two was a thrill seeker, and a vain glory hunter. On any fine Tuesday in July, you might meet Two down at the zoo, paying extra to ride on a whale. Or a week Monday from thence, it's parachuting from a decommissioned military helicopter, sold off after the conclusion of some civil strife or other to a band of village baboons. Two was known to ring the bell and pay for rounds in a packed bar on Friday night, just to look the big pig for a moment. A fair surplus income was generated by the product of their labour, and yet Two was forever on his knees before his brothers, begging for mercy and swearing future fidelity to austerity.

Two was, of course, inclined to a bit more luxury than his las-civious monk of a brother. On the day of arrival he began work on a beachy bungalow at the stream's edge, with a deck out over the water. All wood, sanded down smooth, for he loved the sensual feel of sanded wood on his belly. Well.. the wood didn't end up all that smooth, for Two was a better dreamer than a doer. The structure stood, provided shelter within and shade without. It would do for piggy Two, though his belly disagreed.

Over time, all but the barest of furniture had been pawned away. The allure of prestige and adventure proved all too tempting for poor piggy Two. He was weak, and he knew it, but he would defend himself hoof and jaw were you to abase him in any way. Two was left with his fine wood erection, that the creditors were sure to claim one day as compensation.

Which brings us to pig number Three, the sober one of the lot. Youngest by a mother's grunt, pig Three nevertheless exhibited a maturity far beyond that of his two worldly elder siblings. Pig Three had grasped the essence of responsibility prenatal. Were it not for piggy Three's meticulous preparation, the move to the clearing would have ended in tragedy.

Pig Three put a lot of time into digging the foundations for his quarters. For two harvests straight, pig Three dug diligently, and faithfully saved. Quarters for pig One were fully developed before the first moon rose, and little had improved since. Pig Two had more to do. But his carpentry was rudimentary, which limited his options. Trotters are not well adapted, so piggy Two had his jaws involved a lot, and what a sight it was. Using only saw, hammer, and nails, Two was lucky to have completed his structure before the first harvest.

After the second harvest, a day of glory was upon pig Three. A deep pit had been dug in a carefully measured rectangule, and proper framing shaped to receive the pour. In came wagons carrying barrels and bags of cement, and a queue of men to mix and pour in perfectly coordinated teams for the next seven and twenty hours, according to pig Three's calculations.

It's true, some of the men spat and bickered about doing business with these pretentious dwarves, these pot bellied farm animals. Most of the party shrugged and observed that pig money would keep the family fed. Some saintly few felt inwardly humiliated that they were being associated with those boorish peasants, and they resolved to prove to the pigs that some men were enlightened, and went out of their way to pay respects to their employer. Rumour had it that pig One tried to mate with one of these type. Quite the hornet's nest of a debate was stirred over the actual results.

A fierce intensity of focus possessed pig Three for the day of the pour, a stress I needn't highlight for those that have felt the pressure. Pig Three had the workers colour coded and arranged in shifts. The pour came off well. One barrel slipped out of control as it was being mixed and spilled partially into the creek. Pig Three worked a miracle in the emergency, and sculpted a small bathing hole into the side of the stream with the spilled concrete. Two and thirty hours later, desperately exhausted, pig Three fell flat in the field, as the men gathered up their implements and shifted out with the wagons back to from whence they came, paid in full and marvelling at pig Three's superb management of the affair.

Pig Three came to under the shade of pig One's deciduous. There was a glass of water next to him. Soon his other brother noticed and came to help revive him and congratulate him on his impressive success. Now you may say that's not possible. But as you can plainly see, indeed it is. These pigs are not bit by jealousy. Pigs do not compete in some social hierarchy, where living standards and disposable income are the measure of worth, nor do they engage in dick measuring arguments. They knew whose dick was biggest, but so be it! To each his own, and the pigs lived in relative harmony.

Even the men on the pour were astonished by the pig social graces. They even tried to be more brotherly to one another as a result, and this in no small part is to be credited with the success of the operation. Though that social altruism subsided quickly enough back in the world of men. Poor Edgar, as they all said he let a pig mate him. That was mean, and not in the spirit of the pigs. Edgar denied this. But of course he would. The men knew what they had heard.

Pig Three came to under the deciduous, and, with his brothers, enjoyed mentally dressing the new concrete structure, careful to incorporate many positive elements of fengshui. Careful with those mirrors! Where do the plants go? They cleverly designed indoor plumbing around the stream, giving pig Three a sink, a toilet, and a shower, all according to principles of this foreign art. Yes, it would be nice. And you should have known it would be too. Doesn't Two's well sanded floor on which to rub your belly sound good? Pigs can be trusted with design elements. No! Remember pig one? Not all pigs can be trusted. See what I was saying earlier about the mirror? We're all pigs.

Time passed. The third harvest came in, and pig Three was well on his way, choosing a false brick look, solid dark wood trim, black out curtains on the bulletproof windows, and deck chairs by the pool. The pig pond, as they liked to say. Why bulletproof windows? Pig Three was a paranoid sort, and security was an insurance policy as he so often exclaimed. One day his theory was put to the test.

We've been so concerned with the doings of the pigs, that we have completely neglected poor Wolfie, our would-be picaresque protagonist. Yes, you know he's waiting patiently for piggy plunder. But I've asked you again and again to empathize with the wolf, and your utter refusal frustrates and confounds me. What do you think he's doing out there in the wild? I'll tell you.

He has to protect that territory. And he's no coward. He announces the extent of his domain with scent, pissing over the boundary of the lot of it with regularity, let all comers try their luck, for Wolf was keen for the fight. The territory is no palace garden either, stretching league upon league in all directions from Piggy Glen. The patrol kept Wolf lean and taut for his nine long years. Those who say he put on weight near the end weren't wrong. But remember he still had to eat.

Prey are not stupid. Prey are well adapted to escape even the wiliest of predators. But everyone slips up from time to time, and as an herbivore in this forest that could cost you your life. Wolfie liked prime rib, and he didn't fear the biggest bucks that had crossed this land in nearly a decade.

Wolfie was the law beyond the land of men. What you do in Wolfie's land, you do because he allows you to do it, a privilege he can revoke at his pleasure. Is Wolfie a tyrant? What do you think? He will kill. But only if he needs to, for sustenance or security. So long as Wolfie is satisfied, then there is no fear in the forest. The leader does not demand unconditional loyalty, or threaten the innocent if they discover inconvenient truths, or red tape experimental, morally dubious, behaviour. Wolfie doesn't tell anyone what to think, and he doesn't stop anyone from saying what they like. He'd love it if you congregate! Throw wild parties and Wolfie will join in. Almost everyone will leave happy.

And you think it's that way because Wolfie lacks the conscious perspective of men? Ha! You racist. Wolfie is a hair's breadth of DNA from you. He could be your brother. But more likely you and your brother are pigs.

No, you are not the brother of a wolf because you haven't his refinement. He is an more noble lord than any I've met. He wields the sceptre with the impartiality of death incarnate. On the land of the wolf, the law benefits the best. All hail, Wolfie. And he's coming for those pigs.

Throughout these months of harvest and seed, Wolf frequented, when time allowed, the tangle of paths surrounding the clearing. He soon came to know those that the pigs used regularly, their habits and comings and goings. He knew every aspect of their lives, and had prepared a psychological portfolio on each and their expected response to critical pressure. He knew that pig Three was an opponent to seriously respect. More in the denouement on Wolfie's portfolio. Wolf bides with religious patience the pass of seasons, choosing his climax with care.

It was an hoary November 9th, a Tuesday the records show, when Wolfie descended on the glen for the piggy feast. What few leaves were left attached after the recent howling of the winds were fading quickly to an arid brown. There was no hiding on the paths. Now, I know your sceptical mind will immediately react. If this plan is so well thought out, then why does Wolfie go for pig number One first? It makes no sense. Get the hardest pig out of the way, and take up residence in that fortress of a house before easily sweeping up One and Two. And again, you disgust me. You're not a wolf.

This is a wolf at the tail end of an illustrious career. Now is the time for his requiem mass. This is not some sneaky shuckster robbing a boy of a nickel. This is Wolf! His plan was Herculean in nature, each labour exceeding the magnitude of the last. Wolf was going to sign his name to his deed of life with this act of poetry. He trotted out of that forest with brazen confidence.

Wolf almost broke character on his way up to the deciduous, though. A bulge eyed wild smile danced across his face for a moment. He quickened his pace and stopped dead in front of One's tree and blurted out the hilarity:

"Piggy, little piggy, let me come in! I'll huff and I'll puff and I'll blow your house in!"

Wolfie lost it completely. He collapsed on the ground, rolling about, in joyous agony for some moments. They were just the moments piggy One needed to shoot out of the hay like a young rabbit from a triste with the farmer's daughter when the porch light clicks on. He was across the clearing and ensconced in Two's bungalow in just a panting dog's breath, well before Wolf had pulled himself together. Wolf proceeded in his theatricals none the wiser.

"Get yourself out of that hay, you fat porker, right this second, and go for a run. I'm going to chase you down and tear the soft flesh from your living body with my canines. Soon enough I'll do the same to your two brothers, and I hope they're listening! I am Wolf, and everyone pays their due at some point or other. Your bill is due today, piggy One."

Pig One cowered with Two in the beach bungalow as they listened to the speech, breathless in fear and horrified anticipation. Pig Three, funnily enough, busied himself with paper and kindling in the fireplace.

Wolfie eventually scattered the hay, and, to his dismay, his shock and surprise, the cunning little porker had disappeared. Wolf had carefully surveyed the field before his grand entrance, and somehow the plump little snack had made the scoot.

Furious at this failure in the first eight bars of his piece, Wolfie chased his tail thrice and gave his head a shake. Then he stood stalk still and stared blankly a moment, a method tried, tested and true to calm and focus our hero. Wolfie pranced maniacally over to his favourite property, the bungalow. This simple wooden structure showed some respect for the natural world, providing for one's necessities without unduly damaging the surrounding land. One should blend into the nature, not try to subdue it. Wolf and this pig shared a dao outlook, without spiralling into One's extremism.

"Listen, you fat heffers! I'm going to rip off your hindquarters and eat them in front of you while you draw your last breath! Your panicked squeals will accompany my bloody feast! This is a message to all in the forest, that the fortunes of fate are finicky, and do not pay obeisance to any of the illusions of fairness and equity you so cherish! Doom is the eventual fate of all, and you will not be an exception." Listen and reflect on the story of the three little pigs.

Without waiting for a reply, Wolfie pulled out a handy flint he kept and busied himself snapping sparks at the base of the bungalow. Wolf wouldn't be able to keep his promise if the pigs roasted, but literal truth was rather beside the point, as just the threat appealed to Wolfie's poetic soul. The more he thought about it, Wolf was happy with the way things were going. He was actually glad pig One made his mad dash to an illusory safety. The best laid plans of mice and men, after all, come to nought. This small alteration made for a grand finale with a three-on-one showdown at the fortress. Wolfie nearly wet himself again at the thought, and struck his flint with such enthusiasm that the conflagration flared up in a twinkle.

How did the two trapped pigs react? Well, pig Two was little help at all. He had browned his lederhosen, curled up fetal, and whimpered a second puddle, of tears this time, to the floor. Pig One, shook badly by the Wolf's arrival, had regained possession of himself by now. He gave Two a good butt in the belly, a nip on the ear for encouragement, and led Two in a race, despite his misgivings about cleanliness, down into the creek, through Three's pool, and into the concrete castle while Wolfie tossed and spun in delight as the flames swarmed ever higher.

Three thrust what would have been a fist had he fingers forward as One and Two once again eluded the lunacy of the wolf. One had to admit Wolf was, at this point, taking his character maybe a little too far. Or was it so? Seize the day! This was Wolfie's last moment of grandeur. A dramatic bow as the curtain falls. A triumphant Wolf would leave a lasting impression, etching his name into stone annals of fable lore for all time.

Pigs One, Two, and Three holed up and prepared for a siege. That wolf wasn't getting in. No way, no how. Pig Three was, among other things, an avid reader of Napoleonic war strategy, and an itchingly paranoid fellow to boot. Doors and windows were barricaded. The water intake was too narrow for wolf. Maybe a fox could fit through, but not Wolfie. The same could be said for the thoughtful slits pig Three had designed, like arrow shoots in a castle tower, for better air circulation. A sparrow might well playfully and enjoyably penetrate, but not a wolf. Then there was the fireplace.

Hmm... That was a problem, and, as we've seen, piggy Three had the fire roaring well in time for Wolfie's attack. Three had planned for a proper mechanical flue to control air flow around the fire, but sadly the Wolf had arranged his attack before pig Three was prepared. Napolean had gained a night's march on him. But he wasn't about to buckle. Not yet. The fire will keep Wolf from the door. For now.

"I'm not the idiot you imagine, little pigs. I see that smoke billow-ing from the chimney top. You are my magnum opus. You should be proud to play the sacrifice upon the alter in my illustrious farewell!"

Wolfie filled his prodigious lungs with air, braced himself with exuberant pride, and belted out with a ferocious joy, "Little piggy, Little piggy, let me come in!"

Pig Three's furrowed brow showed respect for the solemnity of Wolfie's moment. There was a suspenseful pause, pregnant with possibility. Pig Three cupped his trotter about the lower portion of his piggy face, stroking a moment gently, drew in what air he could, and in his stressed, shaking soprano, tooted "Not by the hairs of my chinny chin chin!"

Pig Three was sharply stung with instant regret. All three pigs felt utterly and hopelessly lost at that exact moment. What a blunder. Pig One summed it up perfectly.

"That line really Nucked us."

Wolf was, at that moment, running a hose from the creek up to the roof of the house. He was halfway up a ladder... Hey! Yes, he pre-pared for all of this, hiding things throughout the tangled paths sur-rounding the clearing according to his research of likely outcomes. He heard Three's silly response, delivered in a panicked, dramatic form, the frightened pitch of a pig before the slaughter. But the de-fiance in his voice was notable, and one could discern true courage lay beneath what his fearful emotions would betray. Then Wolfie knew. He was destined to be a legend.

On the roof, next to the chimney stack, Wolfie took a fairly broad stance, threw back his shoulders and his head, filled his chest to ca-pacity, and with a well practiced rhythm, modelled after ripples in a pond from a thrown stone, delivered his masterpiece:

"Then I'll huff!" A brief silence as Wolfie gasps for air.

"And I'll puff!" Wolfie's bass lowered perceptibly, as did the omens of evil intent veiled in his intonation, followed by the coup de grace, crackled in a demented rage:

"And I'll blow......... your house.... in!"

Once more Wolf sacrificed truth, which he found inflexible and unaccommodating, for dramatic appeal. Nevertheless, his accomplishment is to this day unsurpassed. From a full story and a half high, Wolf sucked up enough water from the creek, blowing it forcefully down into the fireplace, and eventually, after immense inimitable effort, quenched all the flames beneath, flooding a thumb of the first floor in his labour.

Yes, I've heard many say this feat is impossible. Sucking water up a pipe to the height of a story cannot be done. I'm not going to persuade you of the veracity of events as I've related them. They were told to me by the very Wolf that performed them, for a task is worth nothing if not related said the Wolf. Far worse when it is not related well, and is therefore not appreciated. An old Wolf on his way out of the world recorded his legacy, for all to ponder the worth of the Wolf and his ways.

The pigs within could not be characterized as a group anymore. We may share our joys, but our sorrows are ours alone. Pig Three dashed to and fro pulling drawers from their slots, banging cupboard doors, rummaging closets in wild desperation, and when he finally opened the fridge with one last dolorous hope, pig Three finally broke down and crumpled to the floor in a piggy heap, squealing for mercy from the heavens.

Pig Two was an oddity. Though I suppose, with all three reacting differently and no comparable situation from which to collect a data set and make predictions, then each one must be considered an oddity. Perhaps I am the oddity for thinking so, as the wolf, when relating the matter, proposed no special significance to pig Two's reaction. You can let me know. Pig Two, hyperventilating at first, calmed himself down to a manageable degree. He was an adult after all. Two sunk slowly to the floor, dragged himself stutteringly, as one side of him was inexplicably and unexpectedly paralyzed, across the floor into a corner. Once there, piggy Two curled right up fetal, like an enormous sweaty flesh bagel and whimpered softly for mommy between piteous bouts of quiet, but violent, rhythmic sobbing.

Pig One was composed. He had been sitting still since he arrived sparkling from the dash in the creek. Pig One was clean. His mind felt clear. Pig One understood that sooner or later that, in his opinion, black-hearted devil would slip down the chute, and the three pigs were utterly and hopelessly doomed. He reasoned further that, indeed, we were all so since the moment of our birth. The wolf will come and tear us mercilessly from our flesh. He is the shadow under which we burn as the briefest of candles. And he is the reason our light is necessary. Pig One bowed comfortably down, chin on trotters before the mantle, and enjoyed the coral of ideas dazzling his mind with death so near upon him.

The Wolf had carried the game to its grizzly conclusion. Some will savour each syllable, twirling it round on the tongue to taste its meaning. Some abhor gore. Posterity demands we bare our nakedness.

Down the chimney the wolf slipped, quick as a switch. He emerged within a true monster, and tore each squealing frightened pig to pieces, bathing the floor and walls and ceilings in blood, red himself from tip to tail, pig limbs asunder in a scatter across the room, and finally, shaking the clouds high in the heavens with a mighty howl of pride and fulfillment, echoing to this very day in the canon lore of Fairie Tale.

HELL'S PRESS

In a prison does a man reside and while
away his hour. Brief, it is, and stained, it
won't wash off within the shower. Share the
time, he does, with men who seek and abuse
power. Lock himself away, he would, in far
and lofty tower. Avoid the plague of men,
he should, whose offerings are sour. A wife
he needs, like Helen, my rare and trasured
flower.

Preface

Truth and reason are not much in season in the halls of our lords and kings. High above all, they are holding a ball, but only for those that have wings. Gold plated they are, magnificent stars when seen from afar, but all too aware of the lightness of air and just how dangerous would be the fall.

There are few that know what to do, where to go to soften the cage that we're in. Placate the state and patiently wait til conditions create the chance to throw weight and loosen the ruler's linchpin. Others will say, though his morals are grey, this leader is similar in every which way to the last and the next and it's best to look after your skin. Don't fight, let them win.

I don't agree. A leadership beastly and selfish and cruel must be abolished, no matter the tool, replaced though he be with just such a fool as to continue the rule of false reform. A guise often used, when power's abused, to weather a political storm. Time he's then given to further deform the slightest of freedoms we hold. Time patters on and he'll continue the con, til the leader again will grow bold. We'll soon settle down in a habitual frown and obediently do as we're told.

MOMOTARO

Mei Ji

Wild and free the wind blows, but not so free as Mei Ji, so the fellows used to say of her. The fierce swirls of her youth compounded into a hurricane, leaving her penniless, barren and prematurely aged. Mei Ji sought help from the wise monks in the mountain. Mounted ignobly on an ass, Mei Ji would spend three seasons traveling 1900 leagues into the godly city in the sky in search of some magic to alleviate the tragedy of her predicament.

Many are the stories of Mei Ji along the path to her destination, and you will hear tell of them in time. But we are eager to relate later consequences of this odyssey and will not be delayed.

The monks received Mei Ji coldly, yet with the grace of an enlightened hospitality. Those monks in the godly city in the sky will surprise you. They agreed to supply Mei Ji with all she desired. After one night, in a cold, barren cell available to visitors, Mei Ji was summoned before the break of dawn. Under a cold cloudless starry terror, she was led to the precipice of a grave decision.

Mei Ji was quite unaware as to the gravity of her choice. Mei Ji approached a ledge upon which several monks stoically awaited, having brought her ass, loaded and prepared to depart. Mei Ji was presented with a peach on a tray. Without further ceremony, as I believe was the intent of the monks after all, to be done with Mei Ji as soon as possible, for something wicked in her nature disturbed them, Mei Ji tore open the peach and devoured it.

Thus she departed on her ass, thrilled at her success. Dawn burst upon Mei Ji and her heart responded. For another three seasons, she rode her trusty ass down from the golden city in the sky. Each step rejuvenated our blackened heroine in spirit and, in fact, in body. The peach, some say, was watered from the elixir of life, the fountain of youth if you will, restoring one to a previous age. Within nine months Mei Ji regressed twenty years, regaining much in vivacity and appeal, yet retaining the wisdom she had so painfully, shamefully acquired. Almost her most welcome surprise.

Mei Ji bore child along the journey down. Mere days before reaching her village, the child came.*

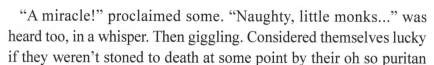

"A miracle!" proclaimed some. "Naughty, little monks..." was heard too, in a whisper. Then giggling. Considered themselves lucky if they weren't stoned to death at some point by their oh so puritan brethren. Such is the sad state of man.

The child came. Mei Ji continued in her old ways for a few more years to build a little capital. With the return of her youth, but the retention of her wisdom, Mei Ji capitalized her appeal. She moved with infant Momo from one luxurious apartment in one district, to another in another and another after that. This time she wasn't such a drunken slut, and socked away a fair sum before Momotaro was five years old. Yes, that's his name. MeiJi and others called him Momo.

Some assholes called him peach boy. They taunted and teased him, chanting the name over and over. That was a really bad idea, as it turns out. Momo was a relaxed and calm child. He didn't rise easily to taunts and jeers. He lived in a realm above the petty insults and slight torments of lesser creatures. But enough is enough. Two boys together got in Momo's face and chanted peach boy a half dozen times before Momo stood like Jesus on the cross, swung his arms together with all the power his little kindergarten chest could muster and coconutted those two boys' heads. The legend begins.

MeiJi sadly departs centre stage of our tale. We're making way for our hero, the unconquerable, the incomparable, the son of a whore, Momotaro. From ignoble births come great things. Plant a seed in cow dung and watch the mighty oak live centuries of principled virtue.

Momo

What? No! She's not dead. Not for a long time. MeiJi is my baby. She's sticking around. She'll still figure heavily in the pages to come. Stop jumping to conclusions. You could never guess anyway. Yes, I'm totally attracted to MeiJi. But not the dirty part. I don't like that. But it could be forgiven. Her tale is not yet told. Not even the dirty bits. She traded in all the wealth she had acquired and bought a double plot lot at a crossroads between the manufacturing district and two neighbourhoods. MeiJi's was Mamasan at an upscale brothel dripping in understated good taste, for MeiJi has an eye for the beautiful. Exploit away, MeiJi, for you are free. Be nice to the girls though. And she was. Have no fear about that. But sometimes these little bitches need a slap, and MeiJi wasn't above anything of the sort, when called for, in her opinion. Meiji was an enlightened spirit.

Her brothel was well disguised as a tasteful, expensive evening entertainment venue, with soft music and slippery service accompanied by a small dining area, especially busy at lunch with the executive personnel from the manufacturing district. On the second plot that backed this property was a guarded complex for MeiJi's home, where Momo grew up, and one or two other surprises. No. Not now. Down boy. Stop. Okay. Just one little thing, for now...

Momo was five when the properties where purchased. There were existing building infrastructure on the lot, some of which was scraped immediately. But walls here and there were salvaged. And something was uncovered. But we'll talk about that later. I told you. Just this one thing about the property and Momo, who found a dull blade among the various farm and machine implements on the yet unrenovated property, in one of the adjacent sheds.

Are you wondering how even a frugal, high end escort like MeiJi could squirrel away enough for not one but two lots of prime real estate, just begging for development in just five years? Or maybe you weren't. You'll want to know anyway. Early in the development of this frontier settlement, a woman was caught and hung in secret. Her story is a sad one. You'll see later. The body was buried on what would one day become MeiJi's plot, and a wicked sapling burst forth from the very coffin. Decades later this malicious twisted tree had poisoned the land. One developer after another was thwarted, as their foundation would rot, termites would devour the wood, plagued by unsolvable moisture issues, every attempt was foiled. The meagre structures MeiJi inherited smelt of failure and decay.

On a visit to the property before her purchase Momo had wandered off. This was a momentous occasion for multiple reasons. Though she didn't know it at the time, this would be last time in her life that MeiJi would whore herself out, an accomplishment and a farewell she would remember well in later years, not for the performance, for that agent was not memorable in any way. Oh! Don't be sad, dear, you were just fine. It's just that I remember the occasion for different reasons. It was a landmark moment in my life.

The agent had eyed her on day one, and she knew it too. He thirsted and she cooled him off. She bargained over the deal with her sexuality and won handsome rewards, learning all the weaknesses of the sellers without ever consummating her promises to the agent. He was led to believe that he would be satisfied when the deal closed.

She learned of the poisoned land and the cursed fruitless tree. Her curiosity piqued, her spirit challenged, her ambition unrelenting, she went to see, to have a peek, a little look. Nothing seemed much out of order. MeiJi was quite surprised, and pleased. Even upon seeing the tree, MeiJi was absolutely certain she could invest in this location with confidence. While MeiJi and the agent were out on one of their long walks about the property, Momo found that dull knife in the shed.

And he found that tree. Momo started in aggressively with that ridiculously dull knife that would squish a block of cheese, and be difficult to do at that. Momo was undaunted. Momo was focused and determined. And Momo made way. Not just through the trunk horizontally, but eventually down into the core, hollowing out the entire root structure at not yet maybe a full five years old? No. Yes. I'm sure. He was fully five at that time. My fault. I had to look back a moment. I apologize.

There's an elephant in the room. Of course! We haven't even mentioned it yet and that's the whole point we were trying to clear up from the beginning. Was Momo a magical creature, inseminated by a peach from the garden of the godly monks high in the heavens? Otherwise, this incident with the hollowing out of the tree has no context, and you'd think it totally impossible, which it was, just that Momo is the god loved son of a peach.

Enraged Momo, with aggression inspired by the gods, attacked the very root of that tree, into the coffin of the sad story witch, and drew forth a medallion, among other trinkets, which was from thence and forevermore hung about his neck.

The contract for the property was consummated that very day. The domain over which MeiJi was to become master was born.

Mamasan

But back to what we were saying about MeiJi the Mamasan. Her authority was unquestioned by staff and patrons alike. She ruled as queen, with a sharp look, a sharp tongue, and the vengeance of the gods. She even had a dungeon of sorts hollowed into the foundation, rarely but not never needed, to cool off the unruly or punish the wilfully wicked. It wasn't long before MeiJi no longer needed big fellas to pound on the badly behaved. Momotaro was a fully grown man by the time he was eleven years old. He caused no end of havoc in the preceding years, having to be chained up more than once. In fact the dungeon was mockingly alluded to as Momo's play room. More on the chronicles of Momotaro later, as you need to fill in the main lines before you can appreciate the details.

No need to fear. Momo was monstrously huge, but he remained relaxed and calm throughout his life. His adorers bless him as contemplative, meditative, possessing a mental gravity that centres his mind, while ours constantly spin. His detractors prefer to obsess over his volcanic rage. Most who ever knew or met Momo would claim truthfully that they never saw him hurt a fly, going out of his way to not do so on occasion. But there were episodes. Not funny, like when you see am emotional woman throwing a fit in the street. Fearful. Totally unhinged in a hurricane. And we'll see one of those times soon enough.

Momo held fast to an ephemeral moral code all his own. He would not voice any principles of this code, but it existed, and when it was crossed, Momo would focus his will to right the wrong. Though it might not be a wrong you or I might perceive, as Momo was unique in his perceptions. Momo did, occasionally, demand recompense or acknowledgement or apology from unsuspecting persons. One such fellow, refusing to apologize for the insult he had directed at a young lady of the establishment, was crippled for life when Momo broke his leg like a green branch with a twist of his wrist, the leg held fast between thumb and forefinger. The man was resolute that he had not insulted the lady, and the lady herself was not pressing any claim. Momo would not relent. Nor did he when another man stood chattering in front of the doorway, creating a jam of bodies. The man was picked right up off his feet and tossed out the open window from the second floor, luckily landing softly in some shrubbery and suffering no more than minor lacerations and a bruised hip bone from which he fully recovered by the way. Many there are and varied the vignettes painted of Momotaro and his exploits, but let us not deviate, for we should be disciplined.

These moments of violence, including the two described above, were not executed with a thundering lunatic hate, mind you. Momo was mindful, most of the time, and was not easy to rile, but when the code was crossed, action he would take. Momo would say he was impartial if he cared to speak at all. Momo was a man of few words, and those few were not wasted defending himself from the accusations of others. It was received as sacramental fact that Momo was in the right in all his moral judgments. Who would dare oppose him?

Not that you would find Momo daily dispensing his own special brand of justice, a vigilant vigilante. Momo allowed the fabric of time to weave about him, as if he alone were unmoving and unchangeable. He was a spider at the centre of his web, feeling the tug of the strings, their vibrations and harmonies, so fully engrossed in the experience of the moment that he rarely focused on any one incident.

But his detractors were not wrong. A plague had set about the land, and stories of the piling bodies of the dead came from cities far away. Then, quickly, very close. An evil pestilence, an agonizing death, always fatal. But one town removed reported a death by plague, signs on the corpse being unmistakable. Momo left in the dead of night and no news reached home of him, or anything else for that matter, for a fortnite. Momo had massacred the entire town, burnt the corpses, and quarantined himself before returning. Though everyone knew, no one ever mentioned this incident, and Momo therefore was ashamed of all mankind.

The meat of our narrative is fast approaching. A carousel of characters arrive and depart nightly at Orchid, ...

What's that? What does Momo look like? What's he wearing? You want more about Momo as a man before we continue? I suppose it's not out of place. But how impertinent of you! Telling me my duty, you're lucky you get anything at all. And yes, MeiJi's palace, the slut farm, is called Orchid. And what does Momo look like? He's a big dude. A big Japanese dude. What? Yes. Japanese. You didn't know that, you ignorant pleb. Momotaro, the peach boy, is Japanese. And he's awesome. But that's only as you'd expect.

Algarth

A carousel of characters arrive and depart nightly at Orchid, and one might not notice a customer in the crowd. An unusual customer. He wasn't there for the girls. Or the boys. He sat alone and nursed a drink for an hour or so and then left, one night after another. Do you think he's some kind of weird psycho? I'm not sure yet myself. Momotaro was aware, but said nothing. The man glanced Momo's way on occasion, but so did everyone. Momo didn't disappear in a room. He was a powerful magnet for attention.

This lank, unkempt fellow with a messy long, but still coloured, beard hanging off his messy long face deserves our respect too. "I am Algarth Oni, and I have a valid claim on property wrongfully taken from me that now resides within the walls of this establishment. I do not claim that wrongdoing has been done by those in possession of my property. Nonetheless, it is rightfully mine. It hangs now round the neck of this Giant I have heard called Momotaro."

A waitress buzzed round our new friend while he was making his fine speech, and he accidentally bumped a table and shook a drink. Momotaro thumped the mallet of his fist on the table nearest, and plates jumped on every table in the room. After a yelp or two, silence reigned, and attention was directed between Momo and our man, Algarth. Algarth repeated his fine speech with a proud tone, yet remaining respectful. Algarth wasn't fooling around, but all could see the beads of sweat begin to break across his slightly wrinkled whispy forehead. All awaited Momo.

Momo said nothing. All was still. Algarth took the two steps unconfident, but determined, towards Momo, "I'll have my family heirloom." Before he knew it, Algarth's entire head was engulfed in Momo's giant paw, and the head was bounced like a coconut off the table nearest, once again suffering unwarranted abuse. Clearly the direct approach was not possible under present circumstances. As Algarth recovered, seated now next to Momo, dishes and glasses were rearranged hastily and without much comment. An tense astonishment sharpened the air. Don't ignore that tension. That's real. That's magic. Anything can happen in such moments, as our antennae are set to receive. What are we capable of?

Momo felt like a puppet master in these moments, comfortably applying the code as circumstances demanded, never experiencing the crippling hesitations of self doubt or fear, and he found that his slightest application of will could order the group, and they would not resist. Nevertheless, Algarth did not relinquish his claim. Looking hard into the eyes of Momotaro, Algarth began, "That medallion around your neck is of incomparable value to me, and, as you'll hear, for many others. It was crafted millennia ago. It's rich in impossible metals, yes, but it has much further value than its mere worth in coin.

"My home is an island at a critical stronghold in the sea, called Onigashima. We were a reliable and trusted trading port, where vessels from all over could resupply, and hold over in a storm. We have been thus since time immemorial. We have a rich local culture, and traditions all our own. That medallion around your neck was a ritual amulet relied upon by hundreds, by our whole community for good fortune, though we knew it not. We simply fared well in trade and lived lives of comfort, attributing success to ourselves and our profound abilities. We were mistaken."

"Two generations back, my very Grandmother was a local apothecary of sorts. Some people thought her mad. The rumours are true, that in my family, the Oni, madness has a foothold. But hers was a gentle madness, and she was accepted as an somewhat eccentric old witch at the fringe of social gatherings. Respect for my family, however, and toleration of our flaws is traditional on the island, as our family bore that amulet as an heirloom. On the solstices, some would pay tribute in a ceremony to the good fortune brought to the island by this very object. It was ancient, and we were the most ancient family known in the land. Not all people followed these traditions, but some still did. Then an horrible tragedy occurred."

"My Grandmother died. The possession of the amulet fell to my mother. Now I must reveal to you an painful fact. My dear mother was most certainly mad. And not in the funny way. She set fire to a man's garden with a potion that blackened the earth around his home to this very day. She wasn't often so violent. She might cackle after securing a glass to a wall with permanent adhesive. Or howl merrily when a bird dropped his business on a man in a park or beach. Harmless enough to be let go about her business in public, but an unholy terror at times. Still she was my mother, and she loved me.

My mother bore that magic amulet round her neck as she was hunted by village henchmen all the way out here to the borderlands of our province. She was hanged and buried here, on this very land."

I gotta say, the crowd was into it! They liked this story. They were hooked.

"The death of my dear mother was a blow to me." Here Algarth, paused and allowed some seedling empathy a little air. "I am forced to accept the official account of her death, that my mother hanged herself. The law was not on my side that day. I will cower in endless sorrow, weeping for the justice my mother never received. I have tried my best." Algarth is not a bad guy, it seems, and so thought many, especially one particular girl staff, who was rubbing her hand between her legs rhythmically to the speech. She was a queer one, and this wasn't her first time, most people liked it. Algarth continued un effected.

"Many consider the medallion the seed of our good fortune as a people. My land has withered since its disappearance. The vengeance of the gods is a fearful terror. Storms have ravaged our shores. What little crops we maintained were destroyed, not once but thrice in the ensuing years. Our ports were torn to splinters, and structures built close to the sea were severely damaged, which is to say all of them on the island. Ships could no longer dock, and we lost all our trade, and with it the last vestiges of hope. Here I stand, nearly naked, before you, beseeching on behalf of an entire people for the return of my ancestral property. I have a rightful claim. My mother's amulet, to you, is a mere decoration. My family heirloom is your vain adornment."

Momo abstains from the interactivity that was expected of him. Algarth has little choice but to continue in some fashion or other. The crowd was getting antsy.

"I have been to this land many times before. Long before it was ever disturbed by your development. And I have seen the tree that grew upon her grave. I have wept for her on these very grounds. And I, too, attempted to dig out the roots of that tree and recover my family's medallion, only to fail miserably. And I was not the first to try. "

"Were you here about a decade ago? I think we met, when this place was a small pickle farm for about a year there. We talked about getting those coke furnaces hot to smelt steel, do you recall?." One of the managerial class piped up. Bob. All look his way, and, for the first time, we hear Momotaro speak... He raises his giant limb, from his seated position points a sausage at the man at the full length of that rock smashing arm and says..

"Bob!", with such command, that Bob was ready to self sacrifice. "Shut your mouth." Momo oozes Zeus's authority.

Bob was a regular with both the executive lunch and evening crowd, that horny little bastard maker. Well liked by all, but his wife and kids. Bob sat down, quite ashamed, realizing the inappropriateness of his remark. What an horrible social blunder. Bob shrunk into the shadows in his plush forest green velvet flared highback recliner. Bob was disgusted with himself, and all were disgusted with Bob. He was sure he could buckle down and swallow the shame, with some gentle work he was sure he would recover, with little but an ancient scar. Momo would not forget though.

"I came again, as you have seen, three days ago. I was astonished. The tree has been uprooted. My mother's soul has been released, that is how I interpret this omen. May she find peace in the afterlife that was not afforded her in the flesh. "

"And I find my family heirloom adorning a monster. I have tried and I have failed to recover my property by force. I am now appealing to your own sense of justice, Momotaro. For the entire population of my island, 347 souls, rely upon your right judgment, Momotaro. And if this is not enough, if I have not persuaded you with the justice of my cause, then let me involve your self interest. I have a will, recognized by the court, who at this very moment uphold my claim upon my birthright, the medallion that is your decoration, Momotaro."

Algarth held peace for a moment. Momo ate a banana while Algarth delivered his fine speech. Now he was finished and politely folded the peel and lay it on the much abused table nearest. As Momotaro remained silent, as was his custom, conjectures and opinions began sporadically, and spread virulently. Algarth in has knatty pants, and long suffering leather long coat, his tangled face hair and his unwashed face has biased you towards him. You think him a lout. How could you? Your disrespect is the manifestation of a meagre, deformed spirit.

Momotaro held no such biases. "I will come to your island.", delivered like a smith's hammer on the anvil of death.

"You are a man of honour, Momotaro. I leave you on your noble word." And at that our mysterious visitor from a far flung land pirouettes his leather long coat, tilts his head and measures a march to the door, and the handle, and oh god!, and he's gone, with great relief.

No more was heard of Algarth. And no more was heard from Momotaro. A half moon's wane and Momo had prepared a pack of comforts for his odyssey. He was off at the pitch of dawn, to walk the leagues of country into the den of the devil she witch cult, Oni. Madmen!

Odyssey

Less than half a day march from Orchid, and we'll skip the fare thee wells and such from his home, bursting from the corn field comes an Haokkaido Inu. The Inu bounds to block the path, skids to a stop and addresses Momo with soulful howl. "Yes," said Momo, "I am Hoki" said the dog, and the bond was set between the two.

Time on the road is long. Between Momo and Hoki was a shared honour that neither would sacrifice on pain of death, a relationship Momo had not felt before. Hoki was a brother. Hoki had heard of the Oni. The island of Onigashima had been cursed these years passed. Rumour told of lost treasure, a ritual amulet that brought good fortune to the island and its people. Momo shared the secret of his medallion, and the purpose of his trek, which wasn't entirely clear. Momo would remain above frustration. He would watch and he would listen.

Hoki warned against Onigashima. The people there are desperate, scratching bark off trees to sate biting hungers. Hoki heard tell of horrible bandits, highwaymen, and robbers. Not that Momo would meet a match, but there is nothing to gain. Momo reminded his friend of the pledge he had made before all, and he would not be dissuaded by the horror stories of a hound, even noble Hoki.

Onward they trod, through days of rain and howling winds, finding what sleep they could under a black dome of cloud, rising each morn covered in a chill frost. South was their route, and days folded into weeks. The cold subsided, and their journey staved off the onset of winter for a time. Arriving on the coast of a vast sea, Momo faced out to the void with such stillness of spirit as to blend into the harmony of heavens and earth. Other men may be seen at great distance amidst a messy muddled landscape. Momo was masked in the most naked environment.

Momotaro waits. He is patience personified. A statue facing the sea, through wind and rain, as the heavens roll from night to day, and slowly the seasons give way. The brisk chill of early winter bares the branches while Momo still waits, disguised as he was as one with the land, when along rows a ferry boat up to the shore. The

Ferryman lashes a rope to a post and steps with ginger swift caution from the tilting gunwale, but one step from giant Momotaro, whom he had not yet seen.

The ferrymen steps. He is startled. Aghast! His neck snaps sharply back, throwing the hood from about his head, and what a ferryman have we here! He's a monk! Having stepped on the foot of a moster unseen has shocked our friend, and he stumbles back into the water, wet to the knee, and cowering in fear. At first. As Momo gazes down on the Ferryman, his look is not of malice or deceit or devilry of all sort. This monster is perhaps of a principled cast thinks the ferry man, much less distressed.

"Pardon my alarm, friend. I am an excellent judge of character, as a ferryman needs be, and you have, sir, a noble bearing. I would risk to trouble you for a moment of your time."

"Let us sit. Monk. You look like a monkey." Hoki, following faithfully, sat watchfully from the shade of near bark.

"Not the first or last time such an observation will be made. I am an hairy faced man. Mister Master Mumphrey Moriarty Morris Milthrope Macteur is my name. Just Morris, if you please. That the wonder of you went unseen is a worry to an old monk ferryman such as myself. I question my own senses, for you were not there, or not distinct as such. I have grown old and weak, as has the land. We were once young and well together. Travellers from all ports stopped about this sea, and trade flourished. The land paths were worn deep with the traffic of persons and goods, all in commerce and trade throughout the valleys and vales and glades and glens and ferns and fens of the forest, and village market squares filled with all the world's wares, the gowns in the towns and the balls and the halls and the belles and their swells swept through with coin spread sundry in their wake. When a curse struck the land, and we knew not why. Pronounced in the sky that our island would die, we have struggled through many lean years. The crops will not grow, though we still hope and sow, and spend night after night wet with tears."

Sat now, along the shore, our three friends share in the air of innocence, found rarely among men. As the wise rhesus regaled in past glory, then the plummet from heaven's gate into the painful depths of misery and loss, Momo sat passive, permissive, and as always patient, awaiting fate's flame to flicker.

"Take us to Onigashima."

"A rare fare, my friend, I'm pleased to be of service. I will deliver you to the island for your coin, but under no condition will I disembark from the ferry. Onigashima is cursed. For once was an amulet, blessed with the light, that brought luck to the land and her people."

Pushed off from the shore, the ferry rocked gently to the ferryman's chore. The waves lapped intently, unceasing, but gentle against the wood of the hull.

"There is an family on the island, the Oni, an ancient clan. Some say they are primordial. Back to the garden of the first men. I cannot elaborate on this claim, but the Oni have long hosted their ritual traditions. Their creed they spread about the land, and admittedly the land has thrived under their management. Many have made their fortune while the Oni reigned."

Hoki settled to the floor of the ferry, having been alert and unsure for some time.

"In recent times the Oni have lost much of their sway in the villages. Here and there, people still adhere to the principles of their past. But a mostly secular, elected officialdom has come to manage most of the island affairs for generations. Some time ago now, I struggle to say when, an Oni mother, a mad witch, was hunted from the land, died, and the amulet was lost, as were the fortunes of the island and its people."

Morris sighed, paused, and sat, as the sun shone speckled through covers of cloud, then continued with his chat.

"The wind whispers to me, and I listen. I am an humble source and warn you to believe me, but the hunt of that woman was more than a murder. The officials conspired to eliminate the Oni from their position, even if only ceremonial, in society."

Morris oared out into the ocean once more, his vigour restored, certain that truth revealed is an healing and goodness unto itself.

Momo unbuttoned from the neck and drew out the chain and the amulet itself.

"That's the ritual amulet of the Oni, buried with the Oni woman years ago, god knows where! Sir, what will you do?"

"Listen."

"Speaking for myself," says Morris and pulls, "that treasure might very well change my fortunes at last! Blessed be the day, my friend. May goodness be its own reward."

Momo considered. The ferryman lived under the rapid rise of his land, while commerce brought coin to every home. Ancient tradition binded this people to themselves, and their collective faith they focused on one above all. Having lost that one coincided with the collapse of commerce and the ruin of their lives. And here the amulet had returned. The old ferryman found solace and hope in the homecoming of this medallion. The good old man deserved his happiness.

The ferry nudged against the shore. Our two travellers disembarked onto the rocky coast. The monk was paid his fare, wished well to his customers, spit into the shallow water, and pushed off again, receding from Momo, his tale, and the evil plague of the Oni.

Hoki froze. A bush at their feet was shivering. Approaching cautiously to inspect the possessed shrub, Hoki crouched low, pushing his nose into the leaves. A frightful commotion burst from the small branches, flapping and flopping about in a tizzy. A paw pinned a pheasant to the ground.

"Mercy! You know not what you do! My chicks will starve or be eaten, your souls painted black with their blood, stained forever by your thoughtless actions!"

Momotaro, the giant, bent and swallowed the bird in the palm of one hand. "You will live, bird. Tell me of the Oni."

The passions of a bird are fleeting, the darkest terror fading to blank idiocy in but the blink of a sandy eye. "The Oni are an odd lot," chirps the pheasant, quite ready to converse, "with their fires and chanting, bells, flutes and headdress. Their forest forays and cleansing of the ocean waves, obeisance to the sun and worship of his sister. The latest Oni woman was quite mad. She filled my nest with her hair once. My sister swears she put eggs in her underpants. Many on the island worshipped with them. And as the island did well, so did they, all attributed to the magic of the Oni, prophecy fulfilled. I'm not so certain myself. They put on a good show. And their members shared a bond. That bond itself has great value. That bond brought about the downfall of the Oni as well. It's all a little confusing."

"You are a witness to all, bird."

"Hatched and bred on this island, as my mother before me. My first daylight coincided with the ascension of the mad queen of the Oni. The ports stocked, docked, and managed ships throughout the night at that time. The Oni were well respected under the stewardship of the mad queen's mother. Near all of the island would come to take part in the solstice events hosted by Oni fire. A bunch of naked crazies if you ask me. Even then the officials had already seized control of most of the workings of the island. The Oni were a ritual, bonding, ceremonial celebration of culture, presiding over little more than festivals, marriages, births and deaths. The powers of the Oni were eroding by the moon. We might as well get going. Why are we just standing here? What's wrong with you, giant?"

"Bring me to the Oni."

"Alright. Walk south for a while. That's better. Fewer people would come for their rituals, the mad queen's antics wrought disrepute on the Oni. Whether or not the officials managed well their duties I do not know. I suspect they are as foolish and incompetent as most. Yet the island thrived! Commerce and trade, culture and finance, investment and profit fell at their feet. The officials themselves were not quiet in their self appreciation. Never enough for them, the praise, and here were these loony claims of dark forces preparing the land and this people for greatness at command of the gods. Yes, through this forest and over the ridge, drop to the hollow a clearing we'll find."

An ancient land. A bare canopy reaching in beseeching prayer to the heavens. A quiet cathedral, carrying the chirp of our pheasant to the clouds and beyond.

"The officials were certainly jealous of the Oni. Moreover, Oni ritual practice could and would interfere with commerce. Shipping lanes were blocked by floating Oni rafts, and smoke from their fires wafted into trade centres. Not to mention that wild witch and her worrisome ways! Worst of all, this large block of persons all pulled together. They could manipulate voting to their ends. So the officials made a dreadful decision, those fools. A fatal losing blow for the island."

Below in the clearing, a circle of stone. An alter, a dais, a carving of bone. A lady is lustful, if living, would moan.

"There it is. Since the hunt of the mad queen the island's social structures have disintegrated. Storms ravaged the shore. Modern transport has made stop over ports unnecessary. The various coin of neighbouring lands have stabilized in relative value, robbing the island of a very profitable enterprise. Maybe some seasonal cyclical climactic disadvantages have occurred to reduce the yield of the land. Anyhow, the people suffer. In their despair, they band together once again. An new Oni king has ascended! Here we are. Set me there, please. Yes."

The bird released with a nod and a wink, flew into the forest, forever a link in the tale of a peach boy, a much needed friend, till ears cannot hear Momotaro will not end.

Officials

Momotaro stands before the stone alter, the dog at his side. Shadows stretch as the sun sets behind the broken ridge surrounding, an amphitheatre of tribute to the gods, their gifts, and their generosity. King of the Oni Algarth emerges from the dark of his lair and approaches the alter, opposite our hero.

"Welcome, Momotaro. We rejoice at your safe arrival. The gods shine upon us this day. Would you care to restore my ancestral medallion?"

The forest dark held breath and a thick silence punished the anxious.

"No."

"Come, Momotaro. Let me offer you a drink. Come to my home. I will have food prepared for you."

"No." Deep and resonant. "I have heard your plea. I must hear others. We go to the city."

The many eyes of the woods watched. "The Oni have no desire to parade into the centres of office and trade. That would be suspicious and could provoke a security response from the officials. Momotaro, I wish you good fortune, and an open door should you want it. I hope you stay long, but please make one final visit before you depart, to return my family heirloom. Farewell."

Momo and Hoki went on their way, leaving alter and priest in the wake. Pursuing the ends of a promise, for justice and peace are at stake. Along do they journey together, through forest, by river, round lake. For honour and truth and all goodness, for virtue this path do they take.

Paths become trails become roads become stares, little does Momo care, they'd scattered, frightened, from one menacing glare. "The officials are where?", and many did point with magnetic precision towards the path our heroes did follow. Soon there were fences and fields turned to furrow, and structures and buildings, but static, unfeeling and hollow. To the courthouse our Momo is led by a lad, a kindness he wouldn't forget. The lad skipped off swiftly receeding, his story untold as of yet. That lad is you, my dear reader, Momotaro and you have now met.

A courthouse, meant to awe and inspire, is large and of considerable weight. Finally a building fit for our Momo. Would he agree with the application of this justice? We hope such is possible. But corruption, abuse, and self interest are pervasive infectious disease of the spirit, metastasizing in the heart of man . And here?

Open the giant doors, and in we proceed to the halls of great justice. The preserve of our liberty, safety, and honour, blind to our religious, financial, ethnic, and sexual proclivities, and the posts most worthy of our most respectable, so greatly honoured are we at your most illustrious presence and approval my lord! my liege lay siege to your tower of illegitimate power. Our societal structure must realign on responsible resource and production management. The phantom of financial assets not backed by real world asset is a fog, a hubris, an impractical perpetual engine of growth, hastening the catastrophic collapse we force upon the future. An era must end of financial manipulation. Their every move artificially adjusts the price of all commodities of trade across all sectors immediately. Every one of them is sticking his thumb on the scales. Is Momo oblivious to all this? He is not.

Officials are as officials are, puffed up with self importance. The erosion of funding had them snapping jaws over scraps for the very necessities of life. Water, sewage, their very salaries were threatened. Fingers of an orchestral maestro at allegretto flow slow in comparison. Officials fired finger canons one to the next leaving none alive to tell the tale. Then went home to steak supper and did much the same again the next day and the next. Momo addresses the fat old one in the middle, as the fat old one on the left disgusted one by his very appearance, and the serious middle aged fellow on the right smelled of interrogative smug.

"I toiled as no man can to retrieve this medallion. It is mine. You say the Oni king has the right to this amulet?" Hoki was astonished.

"Please record for me now the following statements if you would, dear. On this, the tenth day of the tenth month, plaintiff registers a complaint with a former ruling of the court of the island of Onigashima. Here, sir, if you would, are the essential documents. Before the court can legally hear your case, we need proof of your identity. Please prepare documentation stating your name, birthplace and date, your present residence and any residence you have stayed in during the past nine years, the same for your mother and father, work histories with testimonials from previous employers, then consult your local security offices and prepare a full federal criminal background form, sealed by municipal governance, then we can talk about the paperwork to file your case of grievance and appeal."

A thunderous fist, born of the fire of the gods, slams onto the nearest table, shattering it at the knees. A deafening crash brought elbows to ear across the room. Some frightened few sought refuge beneath bureaus, by bookshelves. Momo utters not, yet the heat of his rage communicates full well the fury and consequence of Momo crossed. The fate of officials, the Oni, the island were kneeded in the fists of Momo's monstrous anger. Is Momo a monster?

Without hurry, small steps and patient looks, our great hero sees through the huddles of fleshy balding blobs. Experts in advertising their hollow worth, fortunes frittered in fraud at their fingers, outrageous narcissism rewarded, aggrandized. Media may change, but town criers live long, and the relationship between media and politic is of mutual benefit. Media then turns to commerce with her other hand, and the three skip down the golden brick road to their mansions on the coast. Others have jobs. It all works. But for whom, Momo muses. And now is a time of need.

The fabled fury of a monster erupts from within Momotaro. The anger of the gods is worthy of legend, words of a violence never survived, horrors untold for unseen, unremembered, but for the gore that must one day be cleaned. Hoki quietly and sadly sneaks out before all the bloodshed begins, unwilling to suffer the stain forever of unforgivable sin. When Momo emerges, dripping in blood, he paces for the coast, to wash, meditate, and converse with the realm of conscience few have confronted.

A cause of suffering has been alleviated for the community. These some several dozen few men sucked resources from the people of the island in taxes and fines and suffocating bureaucracy, providing little of want for the people in return. They are no more.

What will become of these people? Will the Oni bind them once again, tempting worship for peace with the gods? Let them fish and trade. Let them pursue contact with other peoples. They are well placed to succeed without the pretence to power of one kind or another. Is a leadership necessary for these people of some hundred? Do we grow into a useful leadership from some hundreds to some thousands? Do we exceed that usefulness and representativeness at some too many number?

The slaughter in the hall was sung in terror about the town, quickly reaching far afield. All hoped fisherman Wilbar would hurry along and clean those body parts out of the courthouse, and Wilgick the carpenter would bury them out of the way. Wildon could read and would know where's best for the papers and schedules and such, with Wildic by his side, but don't hope for much. We'll muddle by, and no one will miss the officials. Their families went begging, to no purpose and starved in the streets in their shame. For none cared to carry the weight of a child, spoilt, bitter, entitled and smug, with the sweat of their efforts up the hill of time. It feels increasingly steep the higher you climb, though the berries up there are first choice.

The Oni

From the sea Momo marches, to fate's final claim for the amulet of the Oni. The Oni had accumulated after the savage sacrifice in the halls of justice. The young and the women encircled the alter, silently ecstatic their treasure returned at last. Momo approaches, with Hoki by his side.

"Hail fellow, well met! You have returned my medallion! How gracious of you Momotaro. I appre..."

"No."

A stir. A rustle. A crunch. Eyes blinking in the black of the forest, an complicated dao of emotion torments the Oni clan. Fear, for the fate of the officials was known. Hope, for the amulet has returned.

"I return to the Orchid. You may come. Correspond with the people. Return before a year. Your future is secure. The amulet is spurious temptation for you. I have earned it, I will keep it. What is earned must not be taken away. Work and you will be well." Hoki rolled over in disbelief.

Algarth the Oni king considered his prospects. Momo could not be compelled, that was certain. Stay and manage, replacing the insidious officialdom with a moderate blend of theocratic autocracy. Enticing. But being Oni still had meaning to Algarth. "I will come."

The island of Onigashima was left to fare as she would, through the winds, waves and seasons of a year, their king following faithful to the core of his ancient tradition. What of Algarth? He is no fool. He knows there is much he does not know. He believes in his experience. He has been taught that the land profits from the presence of the medallion. It is a mistake. But this belief spreads, like a virus. For many, this virus is actually beneficial. Quite pleased to be told what is what, not wanting to question established authority, which they take for evidence, they allow themselves led. Do they suffer for doing so? No. There is a bond, a kinship in the clan. A ready community, holding one's hand through the storms and tremors of life. They are well compensated.

Algarth was no fool. He knew what he didn't know, and he didn't know that the amulet brought good fortune. Yet his forefathers had done so and those before that yet again, he, Algarth would not break the great Oni tradition, centuries of their history, to his fickle and uncertain misgivings.

Invited as he was he would follow the fate of his family charm, the seed of his family tree. The people could carry on the traditions, his family spread wide with uncles and cousins, as is so in small communities of time gone by. He could be replaced by a brother, or, eventually, his daughter. Sad, though, were he not to recover the amulet.

"Momotaro, great giant, before we board this ferry. Perhaps I am hasty to commit. I, too, have home and family. You will never give me the amulet. I understand. Come back to my home. Let me crown you king of the Oni. Then you may depart with the amulet, and the good fortune of our people will be secure in you."

Momo is inscrutable. We can only guess as to limitless tides that swell beneath his surface. Perhaps he had a good opinion of Algarth. Whether his mad preachings were a paralyzing irrational poison to the people, or a salve and cure for their suffering was due much to Algarth himself, and not so to the creed and philosophy he spread. Some following him in his inheritance of this mantle may be harmful. But that may well be said of an elected, representative group. For now, under present circumstances, Algarth was, perhaps, worthy of such leadership. Perhaps Momo was happy to be crowned king of the Oni. Perhaps he was tired after his mass murder.

Momo and Algarth turned from the water, and began the walk back to the Oni lair. Hoki thinks something is wrong. Algarth walks quickly, with anxious hope, and soon they are back before the alter, to the cautious surprise of those who saw, spreading infectiously amongst the clan. More and more follow.

"I, Algarth, am Oni!" our boy proclaims, and palms rub vigorously in response. "And I will stay with the people. Our ancient medallion, that precious portal to the good will of the gods, will depart with Momotaro. The Oni will shelter beneath his enormous strength in spirit not in person, as I pronounce Momotaro King of the Oni. His good fortune will harbour our own. May the gods find affection for our great King."

Each among the men and women searched within his soul for a path forward. This new King was fearsome. The amulet would be safe under his protection. The amulet was of the Oni. Palms rubbed in appreciation. Then a mistake was made. Several enthusiastic acolytes rushed forward to Momo, and grovelled at his feet. Another shook in spasms, one more in tongues, a third in dance, and behind him chants of ooga ooga caught fire.

The thunderous fist of the gods hammered heat into the alter of stone, quaking the very earth beneath their feet. "No!", boomed stern Momo. This impressive feat encouraged the excited into a frenzy, and Momo's fury would not be restrained. A savage blaze set Momo marauding amongst the acolytes, tearing heads from bodies, crushing others under foot, hurling women and children into the forest, leagues beyond the treeline, till all scattered, screaming in horror and fear. Momo had one final sentence to the cowering Algarth. "They must not kneel!"

Whether Algarth acquiesced would distract us from the conclusion of our tale. The burst of carnage past, horrifying and bloody, Algrath the Oni, harmonizing a flat seventh to shape fate's chord forward, thought only of tomorrow for Onigashima. "Our great King will depart, carrying the soul of our people under his protection. See, now, that we are secure. May the favour the gods shine on King Momotaro reflect upon us in turn." A woman, handsome but whimpering in fear, unsteady on her feet, emerges from the Oni lair. Algarth beckons. She is his wife. Delicate and graceful in what movement she could control, yet sniffing and snivelling, as the sight of a decapitated, though familiar, body still leaking upset her. Her shaking arm offered a sack to unmoving King Momo. "Millet dumplings. You will be hungry." Momo received the offering. And departed.

Not steps from the treeline, his homeward journey just begun, an alarmed oof chirps as Hoki paws up a trunk, one branch up upon which sat a nest. Momo looks in on his pleasant pheasant friend. "Great Momo! Thank you for the culling. The humans were an infestation, my friend. The fowl of the island heartily approve!" Momo leaves a goodly portion of millet dumplings for the pheasant and her family. And departs.

Momo boards the ferry with the calm of the deepest ocean recess. The obliging monk is grateful for the fare. "You've saved me half my pocket, good sir! The financial assault of those thieving officials was beggaring the people. When I heard of your murders, I hurried along to the courthouse and dyed one of my shirts in their blood." Knudging the far shore, Momo disembarks, pays his fare, and leaves a goodly portion of millet dumplings for the monk, may he prosper. And departs.

Hoki and his loyal companion, the unfathomable giant Momotaro have a journey before them of pleasant repose into a blossoming spring of universal peace.

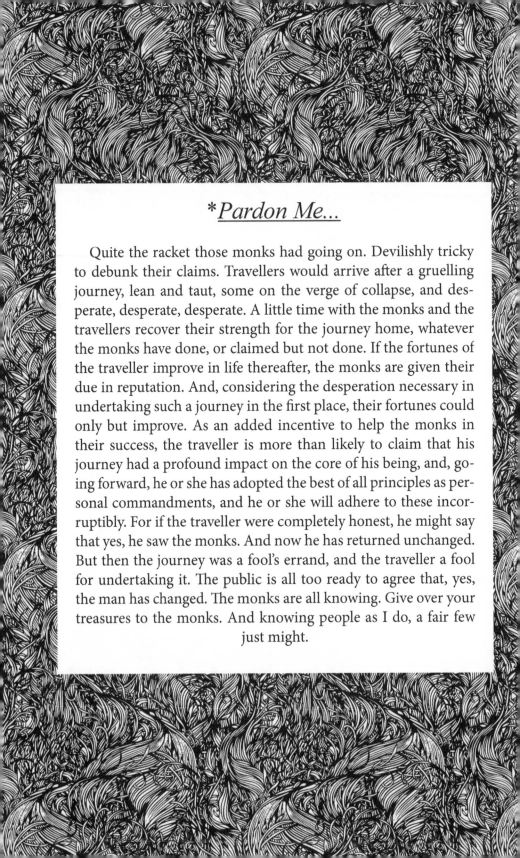

*_Pardon Me..._

Quite the racket those monks had going on. Devilishly tricky to debunk their claims. Travellers would arrive after a gruelling journey, lean and taut, some on the verge of collapse, and desperate, desperate, desperate. A little time with the monks and the travellers recover their strength for the journey home, whatever the monks have done, or claimed but not done. If the fortunes of the traveller improve in life thereafter, the monks are given their due in reputation. And, considering the desperation necessary in undertaking such a journey in the first place, their fortunes could only but improve. As an added incentive to help the monks in their success, the traveller is more than likely to claim that his journey had a profound impact on the core of his being, and, going forward, he or she has adopted the best of all principles as personal commandments, and he or she will adhere to these incorruptibly. For if the traveller were completely honest, he might say that yes, he saw the monks. And now he has returned unchanged. But then the journey was a fool's errand, and the traveller a fool for undertaking it. The public is all too ready to agree that, yes, the man has changed. The monks are all knowing. Give over your treasures to the monks. And knowing people as I do, a fair few just might.

HELL'S PRESS

In a prison does a man reside, a shell, a mortal coil. Live, he does, if one did ask, a life of constant toil. Plead, he will, when times are tough, in Hell too soon to boil. Meet, he must, before he does, the Liars only Foyle. Annointed will he be that day with Heaven's sacred oil. Hell's grand feast for when he comes is all too sure to spoil.

Preface

Merit is a metric not so clearly understood. We think the gifts of fortune are all doled out to the good. But we're wrong, oh very wrong, you've got your head stuck in a hood. Fortune doesn't care what you can measure with a stick. The stupidity contained within that thought just makes me sick. Fortune, you will find if you've missed it as of yet, is handed out in gobs to the most capable bootlick.

Others try to force Dame fortune over to their place. But she can't be manipulated, that's just not the case. Yes, she bends to preferences, but she will not be leashed. Careful lest you push too hard and vengeance is unsheathed. Be cautious when you call her out to make her look your way. She's just as like to strike you down if on your knees you pray.

But sometimes it will all work out, and good will overcome. It doesn't happen every time, but fortune smiles for some, and who can tell what pricks her ears and brings her to your side? What will fortune ask for if she is to be your guide? I'll tell you this, you can't be sure of anything you try, and that fortune favours who she likes, she will not be denied.

CINDERELLA

Omen

"Sire!" popped Bedoll's arm up, hand flung high, bad finger pointed into the blue. The prince balled up the sky in his eye, and saw the great prophet of the gods soar in stillness across the heavens. At that very moment, not several seconds later, but just then as he looked skyward at the behest of Bedoll, the gods let fall from the heights of the stars an omen, a symbol, a gift and a call, a beckoning of fate towards the fields of fabled lore. Prince Lasker sought desperately to find the fifth to fate's root so that the vibration of his string would be in harmony with the all. Our sound survives, an eternal ripple in the fabric, a name that will never die.

Thus Prince Lasker traced heaven's sent with breathless focus, his pupil's filled the balls to black. Flipping in the gentle ebbs and flows of current falls the simplest of footwear, a dainty sandal, as might be worn in the market, or even out in the fields by the good folk of the vale, and, guided by fate's fickle hand, collides flush sole flat on the lap of Prince Lasker. "Sorry, sire!" says our Bedoll, and flicks the unclean item from the cart of the king.

"Bedoll, you bloody fool! Fate smacks you in the face with an omen and you thoughtlessly toss it in the mud, you cud chewing farm animal! Get that sandal!" Bedoll tried his best to exit the cart, but the manoeuvre was made difficult, Lasker pounding away at his limbs with the king's cane. Bruised and battered, Bedoll rolls from cart to earth, scrambles to the side of the road and retrieves the fallen footwear.

"Ah! You'd think it a child's, it's of such a dainty size. At the very moment I looked up, Bedoll! It falls from the eagle's mouth, from Zeus or Odin or one of the others himself. Or herself! Is it fortune? Is it doom? What am I to do, Bedoll? Much too small for either of us, Bedoll, I must find the owner of this fine foot! Call the ministers, sound the alarm, all hands on deck, bring in the king's guard, the army even! Bedoll, get out of this cart and search the farms nearby. Bring them to me, all the women. Let me take fate by the foot, not the hand. We have been preparing our whole lives for this moment, Bedoll!"

A hefty shove from the heel of a burgundy thigh high tanned leather royal boot sends Bedoll once again to the dirt of the king's road, and before Bedoll recovers his footing, the cart is rattling off towards the castle, demented in directionless action, an instinctual response to fate's call, and therefore never wrong.

King Lasker insisted upon a cold and clinical education for his son. Masters in oration, rhetoric, alchemy and astrology were sought from within the realm, the King knowing his people to be most able in these skills. Men of fame for their abilities in physics and chemistry, logic, jurisprudence, governance, and arithmetic were brought from far off lands, speaking strange tongues, unknown amongst the king's people. They stayed for some years and couldn't but help acquaint the young prince with our wondrous variety. As a result Prince Lasker was perfectly comfortable amongst men, wherever from they be, yet woefully understudied in some irrelevant nuances, those studies being not much admired amongst his own kind anyway. Prince Lasker was considered a genius by any opinion publically announced. Along life's merry path, the prince acquired an addictive teeth grinding angst for omen. He longed for the touch of the gods to guide his step. And here he had been touched by godly footwear.

The Step Mother

Round the hearth they gather, huddled together, sitted and praying, their shoulders swaying to the pulse of a demon channelling his semon and Nuck through the neck of each seated witch into vibration, an aural incantation, a witch's elation erupts in a yip of hate! The quiet sets in and the women, the coven, withdraw to reflect on the foulness of fate.

After an hour of rest the mother sets out, shielding herself from the tense desperation of her two daughters. Through the tangled streets and lanes the witch will weave, into the very splendour of wealth and title. A widow she was and all well knew, her husband had died from an horrific flu. So the doctor said, but he wasn't quite sure. Something wasn't right, something impure and sinister. And now she's received amongst all once again. Her days of the black have now come to an end. Act she must, for her funds won't last. A husband she'll catch, but she must hook fast. Each day her attraction so slightly it fails, and you have to look right if you hope to hook whales. She's come with intention, a purpose, a plan. She's shopping for fortune in the form of a man.

And find him she does! An estate by a lake, a forest out back, a cart she might take. Not the wealth of a duke, but comfort instead, meat with her supper, butter on her bread. Enough to present to the public her girls, invited to balls, where the two might whirl with those belonging to the upper set. The mother's ambition would set them up yet. The man was but nothing, he inherits the lot, with some nominal title that the court has forgot. A daughter he has, Ella her name, you know her by another, the source of her fame. Calm down and be patient, this meal will be served. You will be fed with the treat you deserve.

A life of modest indulgence was enjoyed by all that mattered. Ella's father died, leaving all he had to his wife of less than a year, heart attack assumed the local apothecary, the doctor engaged for the moment with an horrific birth of a monster. In truth the wicked coven had conspired in murder and delight. The grave was pre-dug. In some witchy wickedness, the corpse was interred standing up, the narrow hole an astonishing thirteen feet deep, like a post or a pillar, a crux on the east, where the evil winds blow.

And what of the daughter? Keep her, a slave. She'll cook and she'll clean, and have the beds made. She'll know the way you like how dinner is laid. She'll scrub and she'll fetch and roll over and play. She'll mend and tend and off she'll be sent to suffer the hours in errands we've spent. Lock her in the cellar and I'll keep the key. And perhaps from her labour we'll gather a fee. There must be some way to profit from her toil. She'll dig and she'll seed and she'll nourish the soil! A garden we'll keep, and some sheep and a cow. Goats and some chickens, a horse and a sow. Lots of farm animals Ella will raise. We'll fill her life full so she'll not feel malaise. Her life will be hard, but saintly and true. Her soul will not suffer as her body will do. We'll leave her this comfort to soothe her in plight, for we can't escape the balance between the dark and the light.

A candle each month, a cloak and some hay, however will you thank us, Ella? We'll have to find a way! Then she's booted down the stairs in a splendid bit of fun. Or she's first to go in a game they play, called slap her face and run. They pull her hair, her clothes they tear, they push and punch and swear. But Ella took the higher ground, and seldom does she care about the tortures they performed on her, she breathed a freer air. Ella held aloof from all, considered them a selfish herd, their lust and greed and sloth and hate, ambition all absurd. In nature Ella found her peace, and all her love returned by the trees and plants and animals, whose secret lives she learned.

Ella listened to the blackbird's cry, up in the canopy. He wondered whither true love lay? Where could his soulmate be? The rabbit, still within the brush, is tense in mortal fear. Something triggers startled shock amongst a pack of deer. The eggs are wary in the nests of snake and fox and rat. Something wicked this way comes, presaged by the bats. All the forest feels a curse has set upon the land. The witches are a darkness. They are Nuck's left hand.

One night, under the blood of a red moon, the sisters went too far. Ella had curled before the hearth to rest a little while. All was quiet as Ella slipped into the misty sleep of the elves, dreaming lightly of pixie dust and hobgoblins. Suddenly she was sprinkled in a spicy puff of pixie poison, and awoke in great alarm as ashes from the hearth had been swept upon her cloak! On fire she burned in horror, screaming panic, mercy, please! Pushed down onto the floor she was and rolled about in mirth. Cinder ashes covered Ella tip to toe from the dying hearth.

Cinderella! And the myth was born. The name will ring immortal, Ella covered in ash. A pantheon we've built in honour to our gods, and Cinderella proudly takes her place. Fate has played her foul thus far, the girl with the pretty face. The mother dies in Ella's birth. She's born one foot in hell. Her father loved her, felt her worth, but now he's dead as well. Ella's now some property an evil witch does own. Feed the flock and fix the house, they work her to the bone. A crust of bread, some rotten fruit, poor Ella's getting thin. A young woman now, of ten and eight, as the formal tale begins.

The Loss

Mother lifts the latch, grips the cellar door, both hands, plants a foot on the wall beside, and with a mighty tug the solid oak gives way, enough to free poor dirty Ella from the dark for another day of labour. "Out with you this instant! You filthy wretch! Bathe in the river before you return to the house. You stink of cellar air. You'd better empty those buckets from down there."

"Yes, step mother." Ella curtsies with the grace, the charm of perfect inner calm. How might one survive such horrors? Fate's tuning fork alone can suffer such calamity with unremitting resolve. Our Ella is of more rugged stuff than others may suppose. She scurries now from her darkened den to the light and sun and air.

Mother calls up to the girls, insistent so it seems. They're women now, and act as such, but not the sort that dreams are made of, but shrill and vexed and mean. Down they come at mother's wish, frightening bugbugs of beings bombarding the room with their coarse ill tempered vulgarities, upending an always fragile peace. "Sit." Broken to their mother's command, they did.

"Ow! You ass touching sticky scab! Hazel yanked on my hair! Mother! Cut her finger off!"

"Deirdre poured rancid melted butter in my shoes last week, and we're not even! That dirty disease put her tongue in a frog's hole last summer. Nuck you, Deirdre."

Mother alleged an errant attempt at an aggressive mosquito, but all know she meant the blow smacked across two frenzied faces, one a little chubby, one not, with one swat.

"Hazel and Deirdre. Fortune smiles, yet I know not why. A ball at the palace! We won't be shy. Paint yourselves thick and show quite a lot. Slut yourselves up, girls, it's all you've got."

"The prince likes a girl I've heard, a little bit thick."

"I'll sure give him a chance to ride this stick!"

"Send Ella this way, give her a good roar. Tell her today we're going to need a little more"

"Ella has enough to do with all of her chores. She'd hinder your look with her morals and mores. You'll do ok by yourselves, I want you looking like whores. You're bound to catch something with cash that way. Once you've brought him home, we'll compel him to stay." Mother gives commands and the girls acquiesce. In the coven of these witches it is Mother knows best.

We left Ella on a scurry, off to bathe. Sounds like a good time to catch up. Ah, just in time. And now see! She's just so enchanting, alluring, appealing and gay. She plays in the river, she laughs as she sits amongst all the friends that gather in fits. The fish all adore her, she spreads out some seed. She grabs a fish and tosses it out into the air, where a gull flies by and captures it in an acrobatic scare. The fish will forgive her, that was Phil, he's a Nuck. But while she was playing with pond frogs and ducks, like a comet on course swoops the prophet of the gods, our eagle, and snatches a sandal from the riverside in his golden beak. In the blink of an eye, an ah of surprise, the bird disappears into the blue of the sky.

"My Nucking sandal!" exclaims our Ella, and immediately bemoans the influence of her keepers.

The Bond

Her frock is still wet, but it dries as we go, and go does Ella, though in a frenzied torment over the fate of her poor footwear. Unaware of her surrounding, through a forest she must pass. Sprites and pixies, elves and Heather, leprechauns may her harass. Wicked creatures, seldom seen, are hiding in the bark. Stories told will make you fear of what happens after dark. Ella's slowing, the torture showing of her sadly missing shoe. Cuts and scrapes and juice and thorns have made her foot all red and blue. Never fear Miss Ella, dear, the forest will provide. Owl and fox and skunk and ferret, all are on your side. Here comes a mouse, he looks very honest, he offers to show you the way to a house of a monster just over yonder that's likely to help if you pay.

"All right", says our Ella, "I'll give it a shot. A monster might help, or perhaps he might not. But I'm in need of some luck. I'm not short on pluck, I'll knock on the door, I've seen horrors before, and the stars are in my favour this day."

The mouse skips in scattered sniffing all across the forest floor. But give her time and she will lead you to the very door of the monster in the valley of which you've heard tell before. The night that poor Ella lost father forever the doctor was oughtwise engaged. This monster was born on that night long ago, a violence and curse of Nuck's rage. The mother had broken a deal she had spoken to give her first child away. When the mother refused, Nuck's minion ensued to rip his own person apart. Nuck used the witches to summon a demon, and shaped him into a heart. In mother he's planted while she and he panted, the mother would serve as a cart. Inside her it grew, and the girl knew no better. But during the birth she learned life's worth as her end was spelled out with loud letters. Each scream and each moan a word or a thought, for the mother must atone for the wrong she has wrought. The monster birthed out amid a clamour and a shout, the infant to the forest they did send.

Grow it would in the forest it could. Now what do we find, first of her kind, in the house where our Ella's been led? A beggar, a bettor, an compulsive home wrecker, a leper, a debtor, an shameless bed-wetter, a monster named Heather that resembles a setter, Irish as well, and an inveterate go-getter. She's born from the Nuck, and considered ill luck, but the dark must be balanced by light. She thirsts to have suck on the blood on Ella's leg. Ella's horror struck, but this monster needn't beg, inviting Ella in, so the bonding may begin, Heather makes some tea. Ella makes her plea, and in the end they both agree, a partnership will be.

"A girl from the ashes has brought to me a deal. I sense her predicament. To me it has appeal. The sisters you will ruin, and your step mother as well. A marriage I see brewing in the future I can tell. But for the rest you must read on, we must walk the narrow beam of fate to satisfy all you hope for and you dream."

"Heather, my honour, my word and my oath. This contract we have pledged upon will benefit us both. For mine own part is clear to see I stand to gain a lot. For you, we know, reward enough to seed and spread Nuck's rot. But this is something different here, for you do seek revenge. Retaliation on the witches for they brought your birth at all. A monster in the world of men, hated with a passion, down to hell you wish they'd fall."

"Suck, then, Heather on my wounds. May my blood give you strength and lengthened life. A creature of hell I must bargain with to save me from my strife. For that is what the poor must face, to save us from the grave. To submit to Nuck's worst greed and evil, to restrain how we behave, to earn the home and fare we need, were we Death's hand to stave."

The bargain has been struck! For the darkness must be balanced by the light.

At The Ball

I call on the muses! Paint a picture of a prince's palace! A parade of epauletted moustache. The suave, the debonair, the glitz and glamour, the panache. The columned arches, stained glass windows, a horizon palisade, impenetrable fortress, robed in luxury brocade. The men of gallant nature, handsome, tall, and strong and broad.

The servants smart and silent, an imperturbable facade. The lights are bright, the diamonds ever glowing, making an kaleidoscope mosaic, ever changing ever flowing. Under dazzling rainbows dance the feathers, skirts and heels. Which way she goes her heart only knows as it shows the way she feels. Dance, dear princess, and the rest, whom I like best. The strong and pure, the weak, demure, the long of leg, the big of chest, the happy, sad, romantic fad, the tense, the smart, the a la carte, the many endless girls, there's such a dearth, to choose from here upon the earth. I like them all, with shades of taste, like differing brands of flavoured toothpaste. All good for me, no doubt, I'm sure, the advertisement tells me she's the cure. And I'd be happy with them all, so long as the women wouldn't brawl, unless they like that sort of thing. Just don't bring it before the king. If he hears about our promiscuousness, he'll roar and stamp and mug and hiss. He'll interfere in our carnal bliss. This, dear reader, this! Is the palace of the Lasker King and Prince, bejewelled before the ball.

On the stairway to the building you may pause to take a breath. It's quite a walk up to the top, all at once would be your death. Hazel stopped first on flight two or three. Deirdre departed the climb one flight more. The mother marched on to the top of the steps, swearing dignity was seen in one's health. She stood statuesque at the top of the stairs, trying hard to disguise her distress. Sweating and suffering, well out of breath, she thought her eyes might pop out from her head. She went flush in her face, to the shade of tomato, and stumbled against a near wall. Her legs were vibrating, but she held fast, excruciating! And prevented the collapse of herself and her dignity both from the fate of a fall.

Hazel and Deirdre bonded together to tackle the climb just as one. The girls climbed together and met with their mother to the drop of our glorious sun. And here do they stand, this selfish witch coven, like they've just been removed from a furnace or oven. They sweat profusely, but recover in time. The guests file before them, all kinds from all over, in an endless resplendent gay queue. An half hour passes when harks, calls and screams crescendo with the arrival of an frightening squawking, chirping phantom cloud of feathered friends.

In wonder the witches marvel, then recoil in sudden surprise as the mass lowers in flight but soars into deafening shrieks. All at once the flock scatters off into all directions of the compass, the roar diminishes into a gentle laugh of gaiety and mirth, leaving perched upon the palace stage an miraculous immaculate birth. Who is this stunning, dripping beauty diamonds, grace and shapely bootie? Welcome! Welcome to the ball! Entice, seduce, enchant, enthral! In she flows like a petal blown. The seeds of fate are forever sown, the lives we live are only on loan, as fate will claim us as her own one day, for we will die. Some lucky few, before death is due to fate will turn their eye. Let her whisper in your ear, an aroma fills the air, there's a taste that something's near and when you follow her a way to where you needs must be, her touch will as much as say "Yes, my love, I am here for you." Ella's at the ball.

Prince Ponder

"Where can she be? Oh, where can she be? Where art thou, my beautiful flower? Fate, gift me the sight of my beloved this night and I'll swear to do right and act good and not fight, my own selfish purpose will haunt you no more, I'll reform so completely, straight down to the core. Oh! This pleading and begging is such a bore! Such a chore! Just give me the woman, damn fate! It's this waiting, and waiting and nothing I hate!"

"Sire, we'll find her, be patient, at last. We're looking, they're coming, so many, it's one day! We dragged them from villages, some quite a long way."

"Bedoll, my good man, you have the soul of a saint. Pure and un-blemished, with nary a taint on your character too. But might you feel differently had fate touched you? Half the day I saw girls, at nine hundred an hour. But I hate it! Bedoll. The search is all sour. This ball will be better, we'll see less who are fat. Bedoll, this shoe's small, you know better than that. Stop bringing the big ones. Or the ones whose chests are all flat. I'm sure that my princess will be quite a prize, with luxurious hair, and muscular thighs. And the smell of her skin and the green of her eyes, she's shapely and thin, she wel-comes my tries to kiss her and hold her and pat her and purr. Oh my god, Bedoll, can you believe it? Look there! That's her!"

"I see her, Sire, in the centre, resplendent and gay. She's coquett-ish and coy, but smiles and likes to play. She's perfect, go get her! There's no time to lose." But Bedoll needn't bother to light that fuse. The Prince was already well on his way. A chain or a sword, for no less would he stay. She whirls in a dance, and he chases her round. Just when he's close, another new partner she's found. Finally the prince can take it no more, he grabs the tail of the coat and throws the man to the floor.

He's got her, this girl, and they spin and they turn. That special something in his heart and his pants starts to burn. She's lovely, she's clean, she's thin and she's bright, her legs are so long, and her chest is just right. He's waited for fate to send her his way, and he's got her! Now just as he thinks of something to say...

Just then, through a stained glass window above, bursts a flock of geese, blackbirds, sparrows and dove. The glass shatters sundry, the crash stills the hall, the guests all agape at the cackle and call of the birds as they drop, a feathered melee. They surround her, they lift her, they take her away. From the wild frenzy there falls a great clue. Omen and prophecy, touch number two, just what that was you won't need me to tell you. Our Prince is once again hit in the pants with an most indescribable shoe.

An idea! The Prince by the gods is struck. An thought is their gift, their love, our luck. Between us, I'd say, a bargain's there is. We made them in thought and so they exist. Try naming them all, it's quite a long list. We use them for fancy expressive display, or at least if you're Hindu I see it that way. Jesus, the martyr, he suffered, I get it, we're shit. We should each do our part, our own little bit to help and not harm, to behave, to be nice. A little humility and love will suffice. Through the prophet Mohammed Allah was revealed. Bend your knee to the lord, lest your doom be sealed.

And all of the others, the many untold, the gods that are hidden in possible folds of our minds and the galaxy, so much we don't know, so much we can't see, so far we can't go. We are trapped in perspective, and like it or not, we do have our limits, despite all we've got. And how did we get here in the first place, I'd ask? Our imagination. That is the long lost most glorious, most pressing, rewarding and fruit-bearing task.

A scientific approach is just best, that is true. But don't let that stop you from trying the new. For trying and trying and trying is fun, and if you catch a relationship you'd like to explore in a more formal way, though it's a bit of a bore, that's where we'll advance and apply what we find, but don't forget where the idea came from! That supply must be fertilized, nurtured, encouraged. We are the resource, the mind must be read, for we all form a tapestry, each one a small thread.

What does that mean? What do I want? Glue your hand to a wall? Use an extra large font? No, you ass, find something to do. A hobby, a passion, a joy, a way to be you. And share that with others that like that thing too. You'll make it better, in time, together, and find that the thing, though it makes not a cent, you'd sacrifice christmas, diwali, and lent for the chance to pursue it for love pure and true, and if asked what it is for, what will it ultimately do? Nothing, really, just a way to be you.

Prince Lasker stands last at the ball, all having fled. He holds in his hand an unusual boot. Slipper. Moccasin. Straps, bands, buckles, a heel, open toe. Chic. Cute. By the gods, curses Lasker, what is this impossible mash? As the last call, of the last bird, in the dead of the night, caws out on command of the gods, the boot turns ash. Prince Lasker ponders his plight.

Heather Insists

The flock sets politely upon the tale's path, Miss Ella, a heroine none will surpass. But the truth must be shown and Ella unmasked, her name we must tarnish and stain. For cold is the comfort we feel when we know that fate will most favour the pure. We know of ourselves, we regret what we've done, and for fate we will have no allure. Ella was poor and then became rich, I'm certain that such can't be done without compromised morals, one form or another, this goblet will just not be won. Warm do we feel to our girl just like us that does what she must to survive. For do what we must we will do every time for the glory of being alive.

"The Prince is yours! The palace won! My dear you can't stop fate. But as you see I'm somewhat weak, my power dissipates. I held as long as I could, but to hold more would be rash, when my strength runs out, all I make turns to ash. A deal was struck, I've kept my part, you've won the prince's heart. But the witches go unpunished! The deal was made for two. But what have we here? Well satisfied are you, but I languish, suffer and decay. You'd better batter those witches. Help you I may, I'll give my last ounce. When you've ascended the throne, I expect you to pounce!

"Heather, be patient. I've just met the man. He's handsome, it's true, and marry him I can. But till I do there's nothing for you. This plan needs another turn of the screw. Send him, the prince, to claim his prize. Oh Heather! Be patient, be trustful, be wise!"

"We are joined together, my girl, in fate's masterpiece. I'll send him an omen, one he can't help but seize. I'll send him to you, to your home, to your place. All you must do is rise up, show your face. There's a secret he's holding, one you don't yet know. He possesses a piece of footwear, one you lost bathing just a day ago. When he comes to the house, you must show him your foot. In the slipper he brings your foot you must put."

"Heather! That's brilliant! Fate was in front of the wheel that day the eagle flew down and stole it away. Predestined it was? She follows a script? A premonition I had that fate was steering her ship. But is it all written, she's planned out all things? Or does she write as she goes, always pulling our strings?"

"Dear Ella, it's no secret, I'll tell all I know. Disappointed you'll be, and I'm afraid it will show in your angst of an impenetrable ignorance. All things are connected through fields upon fields, all intact, none of which we fully comprehend, and possibly many of which we do not sensibly, consciously, or measurably interact. Fate plays the fields like an violin, and we are the strings. She is the harmony and discord behind all things. The limitations of our tools, yes mechanical, but much more importantly biological, prevent us from truly perceiving the indescribable unknown of these dimensions cosmological. The voice of fate's song sends ripples that happen to ring through the dimensions we know."

"Whoa!"

"I know!"

"Who is she?"

"Oh, no. Maybe one maybe many, maybe both at the same time. From hell I was taken, a murderous seed. I know all of below, I know each evil deed, its place and its person, each form of greed, Nuck and her purpose, her pleasure, her place. But fate and her workings are beyond all, inaccessible, an uninquirable space. For we are all swept in an unceasing flow of time and perception. We will never know what it is to crawl out from the rush and perceive the flow from the riverside brush. That is for fate, in a metaphorical way, and the what and the why and the who she may be, is not for you or I or another to see, but an idea! An awareness. A humility. An acceptance of our limitations."

"Then a joy! A mesmerizing freedom of expression and wonder in which to explore. The gods and fates come alive in our minds, with meaning and purpose and idea we'll find our souls are revealed in the stories we tell. Let us tell of the dark as well, we mustn't prevent that voice from being heard. Who are these monsters in charge? It's absurd. But I digress. Let's move on, yes? Let our minds swell with ideas to smell, concepts and drumdrums and hullaballos, vice managerial oracles too, meetings of minds where unity binds with a shared flow of time and soon we will find that the harmony amongst us grows."

Ella listens with an appreciative sigh. She opens a cut, Heather sucks at her thigh. Her power replenished, Heather summons the birds. They bring Ella off, filling fate's chord with a third. The first and the fifth, all the sounds are in place, and to the end of this tale right now we will race. Will Hazel or Deirdre play a mean trick? And we all know the Prince is kind of a dick. Will he cock it all up, and make a big mess? What might happen, dear reader? Can you take a guess? Will Step Mother play a flat fourth and ruin the scene? Will Cinderella succeed? Will fate intervene? Read on, dear reader! The story's for you. But while you're immersed, hold on to your shoe. Fate's tune is uncertain, fickle and taut. You might wish her involvement, but on second thought you best not.

The End

Homeward she flies with the birds, on the wing. But the birds held their peace. This was no time to sing. Quietly, gently they touch to the ground, and all fly off with nary a sound. To the house Ella moves, and quickly creeps in, and down to the cellar she sneaks with a grin. The witches no wiser, they've all gone to bed, with nothing of their disastrous evening said. They rise in the morning, the sun shining bright. They come down the stairs, but none feel the light. Hazel and Deirdre, their mother as well, come to the kitchen to spit, scream and yell. What happened that evening? I'm dying to tell.

"You fools! Why'd you do that? You should know what's taboo. To lift up your skirts, and drink from a boot, to pull a man's pants down, to holler and hoot, to fondle the statues, to laugh as you toot! How to behave you just don't have a clue! None did you catch, you silly fat moo! And you! You shameless, unstoppable slut! From the king's invite list you've been permanently cut! You can't grab the crotch of each single man! Don't do this! I can't stand it! Tell me who can?!"

"Mother! How dare you! You were soaking in booze! You were rude to the blacks, you insulted the Jews! Who are you to tell us how to behave? You scare them all off when you swear, rant and rave! "

"Mother! You're joking! You stumbled all over, spilling your drink. No man would come near you, they all said you stink. The asses you slapped, the girls you made cry, near the end we all saw you barf on that guy."

Each disappointed, each pointing blame, each feeling keenly the loss and the shame. To blend with the wealthy is a painstaking chore. Who knows what they want? It isn't a whore. At least not in public. The attention's too hot. That's best done alone. The rich hide a lot. The rules are restraining, just what should you do? Where do my hands go? Are these the right shoes? Jokes are unwelcome. Or are they? I can't tell. Some seem ok, but others are not well to be said in this group. That one will laugh, but those spit their soup. Watch them act, read out lines, like a play. If you want to express yourself, this is the way.

We're all caught in our parts. I'll not blame the rich, though their expectations of customs and manners are a bitch. A mother and son, a man and his bride, the teacher, the student, there are parts we must hide. The man in the park that you see every day, your greeting is formal and spuriously gay. The ritual engagement with the clerk in the store, the doctor, the priest, the mailman and more, we're false to each other by following the code. It bottles us up with an emotional load, a weight and a burden, a frustration extreme, an punishing, intolerable, inescapable, dark dream.

They bickered and argued and yelled and they spat. There were hair pulls and face slaps and scratches by the cat, and just as mother got her angry hands upon the bat, a cart was rolling slowly towards the door. An prophecy fulfilled, a promise kept, fate is writing out the score.

And need you me tell you just who's on his way here? I needn't reveal it, fate speaks crystal clear at these moments of tension and struggle and fear.

"Bedoll! I feel it! The omens! The prophecy! The gods! This is it!" Again, cross the sky, the beak of a hawk, this time, by the east sun was lit. A brilliant wide orb round the sun was alive, and through it this bird of destiny dives. "Chase it, coachman! Follow that way! Fortune's upon us this glorious day!" The man whipped the horses and off they did go, up and down valleys, through rivers below, past hills, in their lees, and a forest of bees, round spiders in trees, and all the dark forces they pass with a please. All feared that fate would drop them to their knees in penitence, suffering, torture and pain for the obstructions they cause that can drive fate insane. The web must be woven again and again if the magical creatures will not abstain from their antics and play in the world of the men. Defend yourself, pixie or elf! Fate will not suffer your tricks on herself. She'll tie you in knots for a decade to come if you dance off the beat to her prophetic drum. She'll have it just so, you stay out of her way. Before the door of the house they did slow, to act their part in fate's latest display.

"Girls! Get ready! Put on your face! Quickly! A cart has come and it carries his grace, the Prince! He's here. Get yourselves ready. Deirdre, quit shitting! Hazel, that food! Cheer up! We must present the appropriate mood!" Mother slurred as she spoke, and she looked half woke.

"Mother! Your tattoos are showing! Cover them now! We have no way of knowing what the Prince thinks and how about a baby on a skewer, with little hands he clings while the crowd is festive and jolly along beside the king. And what about that one riding way up your thigh? The tongue of a demon, oh mother, I like it, but why?"

"Mother! We'll cover you. Here's a sheet from the bed. Wrap it round you like a Roman, yes!, around your head as well. That looks much better, this will sell. If you could only stand upright. But you can't. Just an hour ago you fell. What a sight! Just sit there, don't open your mouth. A miracle if this doesn't quickly go south."

No knock on the door before our Bedoll bursts in. He falls to the floor as he injures his shin. He yelps and he drags himself near to a wall. He deigns to get up, but he fears he might fall. He's huffing and bleeding and covered in sweat. When the Prince catches up, he knows he'll get beat more yet. The Prince started up with his kicks and his hits to hurry the pace. "Oh! That great set of tits! I've thought of nought else since I met her and I'll find her in this place! Gather, all women, sit down in this room. For one of you, girls, I'll be your groom. For fate has sent me a message so clear, that had I no ears I could hear her call. And now she needs me as her crutch. Me! Sit down here girls and lift your feet so I can touch."

At a signal from mother, the girls do their part. An enormous commotion sets in motion. Dierdre, being most nimble, is the start. She hops on the Prince from the front like a suit, latched on tightly, legs wrapped round to boot. Hazel goes from behind, she has time as he shrieks. He knows not what to do with these poor village freaks. The

Prince is the meat in a sandwich between a stick and a porker, ferocious and mean. Hazel leans back and falls on the floor. Now is the time for mother's key chore, and this she does well, the experience of a whore. To an unified harmonized terrifying rant, an maddening, hell inspired, Nuck worship chant, she scurries on over and grabs the royal pants.

Just in time Bedoll recovers his stance and belts aside mother, her hands on the pants. Away she goes flying into a wall. It shudders, and down a hung picture does fall. Bedoll grabs the head of witch number two, and onto her ear he bites and he chews. A shriek and a holler, a cry and a wince, Deirdre's in pain and let's go of the prince. The Prince wriggles free from Hazel's fat hands, he shuffles away and up the Prince stands.

"Good gods! Aren't the customs in these parts so strange, Bedoll! Never before have I seen it, and I've seen quite a range! All right, women. Enough of your fun. Sit down there and don't move or beware I'll bash you like garlic and pull off your skin. You can't imagine the trouble you'll be in. Show me your feet." But one glance and the Prince felt the sting of defeat, until just at that moment he heard from the floor the most heartbroken, helpless and piteous roar.

"Hear! The cellar, Bedoll! A voice! Look there! Get the door!" Bedoll lifts himself up from the floor, and over he goes to the giant oak wood and he stands quite firmly and tugs at it good, but the damn thing won't budge. He gives it his all and it opens a nudge, and out flies our Ella of ashes. She's seen clutching her one slipper from the riverside scene. "My darling! Move love! My Precious! Where have you been?"

The Prince holds one shoe and Ella the other. Looking in through a window is Ella's godmother, Heather, through the eyes of a raven she senses fate, closing, encircling, in a tense focused state. Ella is smiling, but not quite with joy. She spreads her arms wide, seduction employs. The Prince starts to shake, to sweat and to moan. In his pants all can see that he's got quite a bone. The Prince rushes over and offers the shoe. It matches! It fits! Fate spoke and they knew! "Marry me, girl! I don't care your name! Fate brought us together. We're part of her game! Join me in wedlock and then do as you please. For the rich the impossible is accomplished with ease."

"Though I loathe you, Prince, you self glorious ass, fate shows me the way and I won't just walk past. Married we'll be and my suffering will end. I'll no longer kneel for my flesh to defend. Your money will save me from a life interred in service to others. Clipped are the wings on that sort of bird. Revenge I will have for the wrong that's been done, and I must have it now if my heart's to be won."

"Omens and signs do not lead one astray. Insult me, harass me, I won't go away. Dear girl, I am certain, you must! Can't you see? You must submit! And tune yourself to fate's key."

"Bedoll! Up there you! Get a hold of that door. Wrench that thing open a little bit more. Prince, grab the thin one. That's all you can do. Bedoll! Drag the fat one. She has to go too. This one's for me. I saved her for last. You're mine now, step-mother. I intend to make it last. My father you poisoned, and me left alone. Now comes the day I will see you atone for your sin." The three were dragged over and tossed down in to the cellar. "Bedoll! Shut the door!" And he did. What happens now? You must seek another fortune teller.

But I'll tell you this! Those withes had it coming. And you can quit that moral drumming. Ella's going to whip and cut and stab and burn until they die. Is there any need to argue if they should die and why? Ella's been imprisoned all her life and forced to work. She grew up pretty anyway and now marries to a jerk. He'll set her up with money. He has title, name and looks. Finally it's Ella's chance to even up the books. They can't just get away with it, they're witches after all. Here comes the sadist bit. Heather, it's your call.

Isn't that a lovely way for Ella's tale to close! Acid poured into their eyes and cutting off their toes. Stretching them upon the rack and embers up the nose. Why not knock their teeth out with an ordinary rock? Wrap them up in burlap and then throw them from the dock. Pull her eye out from her head, and boil that one in tar. Don't turn away from all the fun, we haven't gone too far! Shut them in the darkness to make them go insane. Your turn now, Miss! Hit them. Kick them. Beat them with a chain. The witches scream in pain to the sound of Heather's laughter. Cinderella and the Prince will live happily ever after.

HELL'S PRESS

In a prison does a man reside, a hope he keeps, a plea. Within the cell he carves a stone, one day to be a key. Patiently, he polishes his mind, to set it free. Unlock, he will, eternity, a forever he can't see. Life is but a tiny seed, it hides a mighty tree. The soil is not dependable, fate's fickle on her spree. Her play pollutes the land with unavoidable debris. Tend your garden well if the tree you'll be'll be free.

Preface

Oddities surround us, we pass by them every day. The man that talks to feathered friends and tells us what they say. The girl that makes up consorts round her tea set while she plays. The northern lights, an aardvark, and a shop that sells berets. Changing names of cities , like Mumbai from old Bombay. Too much oddity, however, forewarns of a doomsday.

Too much, I've heard, we have right now, it's climbing up the chart. Much too much contributed, I've more than filled my part. The odd I serve may sting a bit, may taste a little tart, but oddity is what I like, the odd I help impart. Accused I am of wickedness, and far too black a heart. I consider oddity a pleasant niche of modern art.

Here we have a frog that dreams of ruling strict and mean. A cat, as well, improves his lot, and fears not the obscene. In Fairie Tales such happenings are all far too routine. You only think it strange because it's something you've not seen. But such it is, will always be, the laws of Fairie Tales, you'll see, are a lock without a fitting key, and can not be contravened.

PUSS IN BOOTS

Better it is to better a friend and draft from behind to the heights of glory.

"There's nothing like the cavalry, son. A mounted soldier, properly armoured, is like a god. I've been blessed to ride in the vanguard of many a battle, cavalry called to charge as the opponents footmen are released. If you're lucky enough not to get stung by an arrow, by god you mow those footmen down. You might be surrounded by three to no effect but your own immense enjoyment. Give me the cavalry every day in a battle. An archer? I'd let my kittens be archers. They won't see real action unless you get rolled over. By heavens, slaughtering the archers at the end of a good battle is second only to the exhilaration of a mounted charge."

Puss could impress with the pen. Knowing his penchant for embellishment, he made known to good and all that he would not defend his opinions, and reserved well the right to reverse a previous position. Puss would argue that when one engages for the joy of debate, he may well choose to support a losing effort. He will yet pursue his task with enthusiasm, venom and tenacity, all while knowing that the evidence in support of his adversary is formidable, and, in plain truth, unassailable. I, myself, have been influenced by Puss in this regard. Cripplingly disfigured some may say. You may find me waving a flag on a lonely hill for a lost cause that needs defending. If that hill is not yet under assault, well I may claim it to be so anyway. Loudly, belligerently, and to the length mine own satisfaction, I may wail the woe of the long forgotten injustices of yesteryear, of fading fetish fashions of famine fame. Not so Puss.

While he relished and excelled in debate, he was too discerning to allow himself thought the fool for his many and varied interests, and remained reserved. While he could toast a room on occasion, and make merry with his fellows, not once have you seen Puss in a puddle of piss after too many cups. The shame you even thought it so! If he had some interest in you, Puss might catch you on your way out. Or he might bring you a refill just as you needed one. The conversation flowed like a plains river. He could touch on small details of your life, like he knew where you had been last night, of a rendez-vous or triste. He'd know your drink, your childhood pet. Then he'd take what he'd come to get. You'd let it go. Why not? No harm. Charisma. Appeal. He cast a spell, and you fell, quite thoroughly under his charm. Then he's gone.

A legend lives on, and we sing for the love of the song. While this brash little pussy, bigger than most, could take down a mastiff, he often would boast. He bragged that he once sat the throne of the king, and showed off quite proudly his gift of a ring. A ruby set staunchly on top of the gold, of a weight that most pussies just couldn't hold. But we'd better step back, we're ahead of the game. Just how did this pussy acquire his fame? He earned it, I'll tell you with cunning and guile. You'll see if we step back in time for a while.

Not an ordinary pussy, in a litter of but three. He was big. One brother, the younger, swore Puss had eaten the fourth in the womb. That brother died under mysterious circumstances, strangled, by the sewer gate, south of the stone statue. The older lived on, moved west and hitched up with a well wishing witch. But forever a blunder would plunder the value of her best intentioned spells, marring her magic and miring her in misery. The gig fed well and regular despite the worries of the witch. A tickle, he'd said. Hadn't met in years.

Puss was passed to a miller in infancy, and has no recollection of his mother. It was out for himself from day one for poor Puss, for who could he turn to in need? The miller was a fine old fellow, honest and well meaning. The family was a fairie tale, three sons and a dead mother. Thus the need of a cat, the miller thought, to soothe the loss of the mere. Little did he know of cats. And this one was worse than most. For his enemies anyway, or where he might profit.

But let us not sully the kitten for the acts of the cat. Puss, as he was called by the miller, was a perfect pet for the farm. He hunted with odyssean craft. I once saw a herring hop from a river to his paw because he asked it nicely. He kept watch for weakness and exploited where he could. The eldest son was useless, stingy, dangerous when drunk, and Puss long harboured plans of revenge. The middle son worked in his sweat in the sun, to bend to the laws of frère number one. The youngest, the bullied, the smallest third son was the miller's most favoured, but feckless and dumb. Puss stayed close, for when fortune shines, if you are near, you may bask in the reflected glow. Puss needed a tool to carve out his social position in the world. This favourite frère would fair nicely for Puss as a stooge in his clever act, worthy of the stage, and enshrined amongst a pantheon of fabled legends.

Thinking much of himself, Puss, poised purposefully on his hind legs, practiced parries and lunges on posts. He was an excellent boxer in the amateur ranks, scoring well and much admired, but lacking finishing power. He was as well versed in the art of conversation. His company was much commented on in the family, and Puss swelled with pride. Yet these skills were but a dull grey when compared to the blinding colour of a Puss hunt.

Puss would pin flies, mid flight, with a paw. His patience could wait days for thick ice to thaw. Intelligent, cunning, nimble, and quick, Puss could lift eggs with a sleight of hand trick. A mongoose, a python, a dog, and a goat. Puss could kill all with a strike to the throat. To hunt was the one thing this Puss would pursue forgoing all profit, a joy, pure and true. When he's on a hunt, you hear what I say, you leave Puss alone, don't you get in his way.

Days are long when you're a talented Puss trapped in the tedium of village life, a prison for the mentally competent. Shall we forgive him his little cruelties? Frere number three, the youngest and weakest and kindest and dumbest, most people around didn't know his name, cause they couldn't care less. It was Herbert. Herbert Miller. Poor Herbert might have his shoelaces cut short one morning, and his sugar replaced with salt the next. His door might be glued shut, or his bed raised a foot in the night. The wet paint in his cap went unnoticed until he took it off to dine. He felt he would die waking one morning and rubbing his eyes with ground chillies sprinkled on his fingers.

Herbert was more suspicious of his brothers than he was of Puss, who cuddled consolingly, convincing Herbert of his friendship and innocence. Herbert shared everything with Puss. Herbert, not clever enough to interpret another's intentions, was led by the nose as if he'd had a bull ring pierced there. Puss would take hold. Fishing was a frequent early morning excursion, and Puss insisted on sending fish to the king on a regular basis in Herbert's name. Herbert would milk the cows upon request. And Herbert would wake well before dawn to play for a spell, were Puss to smack his sleeping face repeatedly. But he might get a swipe across a forearm were he to interrupt Puss in a nap, or, worse yet, a hunt. A hunt which might begin at any moment. "Fuck you, Herbert," said Puss. Sometimes before the scratch, sometimes after. Herbert's arms were criss-crossed with wounds, hidden under some young man fur.

Often just two little words could restore Puss to Herbert's good graces. Bulge eyed, submissive, maybe even a tear or two, "I'm sorry" was sufficient atonement for one's crimes according to the justice of fine young Herbert. Puss honed his manipulative abilities on these three young men, completely ignoring the miller himself, much to the miller's despair, which was well known to Puss. Henry, the eldest, should not be provoked. He was a real threat. One day, thought Puss. Hobart, the middle son, lacked emotional response, and Puss was denied his feast. Hobart's annoyance was a meagre meal for the troubles Puss took in the preparation and the cook. Herbert was the third bear. Just right. Herbert would lose his emotional marbles at the slightest distress, screaming, often, crying, always, shaking, seizing, spinning, spitting, hyperventilating, sitting, wailing, moaning, groaning, sobbing, "Good god, child, stop! My head is throbbing."

And then the poor miller died of a heart attack at fifty three, outliving his spouse by a mere seven years. The three brothers were left to weather the storms of life alone. A will was found among the papers, and after reading it, you will begin to appreciate this miller, and regret you have overlooked his good qualities while he was alive. He should have been recognised for his good and noble spirit, listened to and admired. But no! You've lost the opportunity forever, for he has died.

"To my son Henry, the eldest, the meanest, the drunk, the despotic tyrant, the pirate, the skunk. You, son, will fare well in this world among men. For each man is your brother, at least nine out of ten. To you I give land and title and deed. You deserve to inherit the curse of Nuck's greed."

"Hobart, my friend, my son number two, all means of production I am passing to you. Take all machine knowledge, production and tool, and apply them for profit with honour and rule. Hobbie, dear son, I wish you the best. Work hard, my Hobbie, and in peace I can rest."

"Herbert, my son, you're third and your worst. You're useless and vain and thin skinned and cursed. A coward, my son, you've been all of your days. The cat can lord over you, so with you he stays. May the cat bring good luck to you, Herbert, at last. I fear you'll go beggar or bugger quite fast."

"In parting, I don't want to stay and chat, I've crafted some boots, I've left on the mat. They're a gift, I've made for Puss, the cat." A great man has parted. And that was that.

You've been introduced properly to some of the party involved in our adventure, and their relative circumstances. For the moment brother number two continued to apply his industrial production at its present location, and allowed Henry a considerable sum in rent. Interesting decisions Hobart might make are not of immediate interest to a story about our hero, Puss. Herbert was fed. Puss was not idle.

Up until this point you might have been persuaded to regard this particular miller living in an otherwise predictable trope of an village environment, where the rest of village life, with its physical and social apparatus, are common, worthy of no further commentary. But you would be wrong, and you shouldn't speculate like that. But I concede you do need a baseline from which to establish any perspective at all. With culture, or normality, is that baseline possible? Or is the landscape too varied to establish one kind of normal. Any relationship is normal in a chaotic system.

Each fairie tale kingdom is unique in itself, though sharing similarities with the others. The narrow path of virtue is beset on all sides by the dangers and seductions and delights of immoral submission. While only one path leads to purity, all the many others are polluted in their own unique way. Vice and evil have many faces. They even hide as virtue in disguise. Walk the moral tightrope, friends, and stop pushing people off. I see you.

Good King Oliver, the fine featured, fine mannered, fine ruling monarch on the Rhine, slips silently into the background, without the pompous flair of your usual king. Honour is his due, as his rule has been mild, and encouraging for the people. While managing affairs of the state responsibly, Oliver had amassed a fortune in the castle store rooms. Trade from all sectors increased, his people were productive, prospects were attractive to investors and the population grew. He policed responsibly, but was perhaps a bit too permissive with the crown's control over the kingdom. There were still lands in which the king's rule reached only with great effort. Nevertheless, by the standards of his peers, King Oliver is well deserving of the Good.

"Time for the daughter to marry," thinks Good King Oliver. "Whom shall I pick? They're a bunch of poesies in this stock I see before me. They're living in their own self created fairie tales. Can't they see the nightmare! I want my daughter and her husband to understand as they rule, that our kingdom is always three months from collapse in some commodity. Even with storerooms full, our supplies are eaten through by the needs of the state. I am responsible, but I cannot in good conscience operate below a certain fiscal threshold of dignity in medical care, education, and defence. The kingdom operates near that defined line. And that is why trade and commerce run so well. And why does this Comte Herbert persist in sending me fish?", sighs Good King Oliver as a servant displays the latest river big mouth.

"These petalled pansies reek of ambition, on the tips of their toes trying to sniff higher air, and I won't have that around my dinner table each day until the one I die. I'm going out into the land to find a fine common lad that will rule with honour and grace. Millie, come here now, we'll go find you your husband."

Millie came along, like a good little lass, and they all clambered out in the coach.

But let us return to the unfortunate Herbert and his inheritance, now proudly erect on two feet in boots, the sly and cunning Puss of lore's name. Now afield in summer days with no compass to point them towards some purpose or pursuit, much was yet learned by this unusual pair of provocateurs. Among fens and fowls and foals and fillies and fern and gulley and gorge and glen, through meadow past glade in the valley beyond, lives an horrible man by the name of Du Pont. An ogre, a monster, who stole, fought and killed. A magical creature, not cunning, but skilled. He could change in a blink from fat man to thin, he'd change dark to light in his eyes or his skin. Much more than that he could do if he chose. A tail and more fur, or he shrinks and he grows. An orange or a peach or a dog or a cat. Du Pont could pretend to be this or be that. But you mustn't go near this devilish troll, he's mean and ill tempered and angry and cold.

A hero was needed to conquer the land. As it just so happens we have one on hand. Herbert may enter with Puss at his side, and their chance for success is impossibly wide. For fairie tales end in the usual way, but tell them we must, for they have this to say, "I am your culture, your home and your lore, I can speak for you and let me once more."

Herbert lay, forlorn, at the side of a splashing river, into which he must plunge. Thus he did, stripping free of his final chains and wobbling gingerly over the rocks and into the stream, naked as the girls I see in my dreams. Puss up on the road was conversing with a toad, when a cart and six came through with the king, and daughter too! Now Puss is not a cat to miss an opportune to chat with the higher social class. He could kiss a little ass, ingratiate himself, and then to further profit he may pass. The good graces of the rich can grant your wish if you will just accept the switch from self respect to friendly fish, to entertain and serve as fool so they can laugh until they drool. Puss had a plan quite fast, into which Herbert could be cast.

Puss, that cunning conniver, rushed down to the riverside, gathered up all of Herbert's clothing, Herbert himself still flapping about in the water, and hid them beneath some rocks at the base of a tree. Puss hurries back up to the king's road, straddles centre, arms to heaven, and garnishes with the irresistible charisma and charm, characteristic of our picaresque hero. Black glob eyeballs, puffed and moist, shy the lead two horses to an abrupt halt. Puss can heat a creature's empathy to a melt, which then spills out of their pores. Even horses! Out pop king and daughter, who slip in the leak of their own empathetic drizzle. Our manipulative Puss feigns a panicked, yet somehow quaint and ingratiating, bow.

"My fair and gracious king, Good Oliver, great sir! My stars! My master's in a mess, my king, I'm desperate for a cure. While bathing in the stream, it seems, a thief has come and gone. His clothes, his things, his modesty, he's naked as a fawn. Safe harbour for my lordship, king, I'm on my very knees. A loyal man, the Comte Herbert is, ask anything you please."

"Bring him along and we'll robe him well. Good acts in good faith are hammer to the karmic bell. We'll live king eternal, incarnate in bliss, if we're worthy of the fondle of fair fate's kiss."

Mollie nodded enthusiastically. Puss ran off to fetch Comte Herbert, to tell him he was now a Comte, to bring him to the king, and to introduce him to the princess. Herbert offered little resistance. Having been told his clothes had gone missing, helpless Herbert allowed himself led to the cart of the king, too simple to cover his shame. And what had he to be ashamed of? Millie thought nothing! Along the Comte came.

"Stop that with your hands, Millie! You'll go blind." Yet the King Good Oliver could empathize with his lustful daughter. This Comte was unblemished, tall, strong, young and clean. Herbert was off to a good start, and Puss was well pleased with the blush of the princess and the beam of the king. Herbert was robed in folds of fur, and seated next to Millie in the cart. The princess herself covered them both in a blanket, their hands concealed, not so their delight.

"Follow the path through meadow past glade in the valley beyond, till you come to the land they call the Du Pont. A castle is there, the valley is fine. Let us repay you with a meal and some wine, Good King let us host you, make merry and dine." Puss bowed with grace this time, as if before the divine.

Then he took off at a pace the king would rather not match, and left the king time to consider his catch. This man, this great ape, this statue of flesh, would his thought and his morals and principles mesh with the wishes and dreams of the Good great King? Would he bow to the throne? Would he kiss the ring? All this and much more did Oliver ponder as he rode with the fish on his hook into yonder.

Puss flew on through valley, past vale, into the land of the Du Pont tale. Puss marched right up to the castle door, and shouted out frankly, in a Puss like roar, "Ogre Du Pont, you smelly fat cow, drag your thick head outside and confront me right now! You've been evicted, I tell you, by order of King! Good Oliver chose me to deliver this thing. You get out of this home and accept what's been done. The king's on his way and you'd better run!"

A rumble, a grunt, a shake and much more brought thunder enclosing quite fast to the door. It opened a crack and out from the black came a giant unwashed and slovenly boar. Seeing the cat after hearing his rant, Du Pont broke out in a merry chant, "Cat, I'll rip you tail to toe and watch the bloody river flow and you will suffer as you go!"

In a miraculous transformation, Du Pont reshaped into a lion, roaring and charging at our Puss. Puss ducked and dodged this way and that, the lion was no match for the guile of the cat. Minutes of chase drained his spirit away and Du Pont dropped, exhausted, into a bushel of hay, panting and muttering throughout his rest, Puss thought now the time might be best.

"No sense in chasing me all through the day. You'll run out of breath and I'll get away. By order of the king, you are to leave. It's all here in this letter you are to receive. Pardon the size, as you see it's quite small. The king's mouse wrote it, and he's not very tall. I'll put it here on the ground, for read it you must, but the print is terribly small, hardly larger than dust."

Du Pont was quite worn out, and not bright at his best. He would willingly submit to what Puss might suggest. "Shrink down, like a mouse," was the sly cat's request, "then read, and see after about all the rest." Du Pont was quite stupid, I think it fair to say. Puss enjoyed himself. Puss was moulding clay. Du Pont shrunk down small to not more than an ounce, and Puss, on the hunt, made a bloodthirsty pounce! Puss tore him to pieces with razor sharp claws. He devoured that poor ogre, licking clean his fur and paws.

And how did the staff to the castle respond? As you might expect, they were relieved at the overthrow of poor governance, as most of us are. Puss lined them up straight, to give them a fine speech about the philosophy of leadership and his intentions for the castle, which would now and forever more be the domain of Comte Herbert, and furthermore that the Comte had been so, steward of this land, for generations past, and that were they to perform to his satisfaction in the presence of the king, all might be well rewarded for their new found loyalty. Reaching deep, Puss coloured the denouement of his speech with his characteristic charismatic bulge eyed charm , and a few of the maids wet themselves in... tears.

On anon, along rolls the cart of the king, with the ennobled Comte Herbert wedged snugly within. Under the blanket was unheard of pleasure for Herbert, while above his face glowed a cherry red. The king waxed poetic about justice and law, committees and governance, trade and taxation, public health and morals, education as the founding pillar of a successful and mature society, showing he was not in fact a fool at all. Odd, then, his utter infatuation with our

Herbert. Or is it? What kind of son in law might Herbert be? Incompetent, certainly, but then there was that cat, who seemed sharp as a tack. Free of ambition, he'd be docile and malleable. Although, on close inspection, Herbert was not the strapping country simpleton the king was hoping for, Herbert was enough of those things to satisfy much the king desired. There was hope for the grandkids, could they be but parted from their parents.

"Herbert, my boy, you're a special catch. You and my daughter make an excellent match. A splendid estate is before us spread, what a dish! Let us enjoy ourselves on the castle's bread, and of course fish! Should we find peace and pleasure within, there may come a day when you may call us kin."

The staff were superb, well pleased was the king. He gratefully bequeathed to Puss a very special ring. It once did grace a bishop, somewhere off in Rome. Solid gold throughout the band and capped by a ruby dome. Herbert was announced right then as Millie's new man wife, causing all sorts of astonishment, annoyance, commotion and strife. That tale will sit on the shelf for today. We have put this Puss on fame's narrow way. For now he will suffer to bid you adieu. This pussy has some issues, at least one or two, that need his attention if all's to go as planned, and what you need is a paw sometimes to direct fate's hand.

THE FROG PRINCE

A hand held suspended next to the stone frame in caution, Prince Tartakower stepped onto the sill of the lonely arched window in the second highest turret in the Palace of Muglac. Poor Polly paused as he looked over the vast lands of his father's estate. Prince Tartakower resolved to take just a little more time, one more day perhaps, before he leapt, and climbed down from the sill.

He felt friction and resistance from all quarters. As a child he had been received wherever he went, coddled and fussed about in good humour. As he slept, fed by the light of the moon, Polly grew to the age when a boy believes himself a man. Now he is greeted coldly and made to feel unwelcome. Whatever endeavour he cares to undertake, whichever corner of the bureaucracy he requires, at his most timid approach they immediately take an offended defensive posture, and are so overwhelmed by the present work that not a sentence can be spared, goodbye now, Prince.

Reform is devilish jinn, and Polly was possessed. He was upsetting to the reliable, and therefore comforting routine. Accusing him of demonic possession was a frightful bit of fun, not just tolerated but encouraged. Polly's supposed alliance with dark forces would

one day be codified into a religion by a small confederacy of enterprising young men. an inner circle of capable acolytes who would
enforce upon the public with increased hostility and self righteous
condemnation Polly's godliness. Soon grow their fortune and influence. But let's not get distracted and put the cart before the horse.

Polly took long melancholy walks in solitude, baring his tormented
soul to all the denizens of the woods. "Why have the fates obstruct-
ed me? My ideas to nationalize the peach industry, confiscate land
from the peach farmers, thereby reducing unwanted competition in
the peach market, providing lower prices for all, was laughed at!.
Think of the exports!" Prince Polly proposed a purchase of Peruvian
pomegranate, exchanged for state owned peaches, a straight trade
between nations of product, thereby evading the costs of the financial plumbing along the way, again ridiculed. They snorted when
Polly suggested amendments to early childhood curriculum, enhanc-
ing a shared cultural identity. Poor Polly posed forlorn, arched his
spine, noggin tilted back, wrist to forehead, shivering a deep selfish
sigh into sight. Polly fancied himself dramatically gifted.

His father was Magnate Supreme, a position of unquestionable
strength and power within the realm, a realm which Prince Polly
would one day inherit. He planned to break the land to his will. Dis-
cipline would be imposed. They would be better off for it.

"If only they could see the glorious future I have mapped out for
them. I see waste and spoil wherever I look, and all that is needed is
the fine management of a superior mind. The consensus is the disease! The representation of the people is but a needless irrelevance.
Vie! The day he may die!"

Just then, taking shape from the tangled dark itself, came an elder-
ly woman with a weaved wicker basket, covered and slung in the
crook of her arm. The dark came with her. A cloud suddenly blighted
the sky. A wilt took hold of the leaves as she passed. Polly, mired

in his own woe, felt the looming shadow as a reflection of his own sorrowful spirit, a companion to his soul. And perhaps she is. She is Nuck. And she is a bringer of ill omen. Closer now, Polly was overwhelmed, "Egads! Woman! your breath is polluted!"

It was too late. A hoary palm conjured forth from beneath the cover among her wicked wicker wares a pill of purple powder which she pulverized and puffed into poor Prince Polly's visage. Polly wailed in torment as he shrunk like a frightened turtle, within three teary blinks, into an repugnant fat frog the size of a child's foot. The evil, noxious Nuck gripped the frog in her skeletal claws, and poor Prince Polly's body burst out in bubbles between her fingers. Polly was strangled into silence, and feared for his very life.

"You will suffer, you selfish entitled adolescent. The lives of the people are not play things for your amusement or pride. You are punished to live as an odious amphibian until the day you can prove a creature worse than you. I wish you misery!" Nuck arms and legs synchronize astoundingly accurate to the most exquisite trebuchet, Nuck launched the frog Prince East, over valleys and vales and glen and gorge, and rivulet, stream, and creek, plunging Polly plop into a pond at the far edge of an unfriendly neighbouring fiefdom.

Polly's plunge into the pond was an unimaginable perfection, the angle of his entry coinciding exactly with the muddy slope of the pond's shore. Polly's touchdown was gentle, if fast, but even the slight friction sent him somersaulting at tremendous rotational velocity. He skipped across the surface of the pond like a flat stone, pushed a surf in his wake as he slowed, and sunk, dizzy eyed to a degree you or I might only dream of, suddenly into the murky strangling tangled depths of maddening uncertainty.

He was soon escorted, dragged, really, in a humiliating fashion, and no part of his new body was spared the indignity, to the foot of a mount one side of centre, the eye of yin in the yang portion of the concept shaped pond. One enormous, fat bellied frog sat lord above them all. He was Rana, ruler supreme. Polly must pay obeisance by licking his kingly foot. Dragged, belly through the muck, Polly's mouth suffocated in wet mud. Finally pinned to the earth by the feet of three others frogs, chanting their tribal rhythm, Polly submitted and wrapped his tongue in a sock about the foot of King Rana.

"All must submit to the rule of King Rana." He was told repeatedly, as they snatched flies at dawn and dusk, out looking for a girl, or while just sitting your lily pad in the sun. We mustn't dwell on Prince Polly Tartakower's transition to his new frog life, for that new life became old quite quickly. All the tears and moans and self pity still torment our Polly regularly enough, but there is a life to get on with, and that now consisted of some strange habits indeed. Frogs climb all over one another physically, for example. Polly had a toe up the pooper twice already in a fortnite, and seven times in all in his first ten months, when he stopped counting. But clearly much more frequently than he had suffered such as a man.

About that time, yet another miraculous fireball from the heavens plunged ever so perfectly, as had Prince Polly, into the pond. It was of such tremendous density that it was interred a foot into the muddy bed beneath the pond. Rana ordered a platoon of frogs into action. In their zeal to please the leader, safety was ignored, and, sadly, several frogs lost their lives that day in the dig. In the end, the frogs did recover the mysterious object – a marble of solid gold.

The orb was hoisted above the growing crowd of frogs and triumphantly paraded around the mount seven times clockwise, a wild primordial chant frightening the children away from the violent mob. The frogs with the orb of good fortune held before them began to ascend the mount, towards their King. Rana, sat in smug pride as this treasure was presented to him, and there it sits on his right hand side. He would occasionally give it a pat with his forefoot, or a lascivious lick with his rope tongue.

Life in the land of frogs was unbearable. King Rana was as stupid as he was ugly. The conditions of the frogs might easily be improved, as Polly saw it. But were a frog to undertake an independent action, a threatening glance or burp from Rana, and patrols of henchfrogs would advance in bloodlust. King Rana cared for nothing but the preservation of his position, lord above all. Merciless and exactingly consistent, Rana's rule had been unchallenged for generations. Loyal henchfrogs were rewarded generously from amongst the unfailing tribute to the King, and carried out the wishes of their master with a vicious sadistic enthusiasm.

Thus reform was not discussed openly. Pockets of intellectuals might gather under the cover of dark and discuss intricacies of constitutional utopia, or draft grand proclamations from deep within their dens. But it was impossible to escape the watchful eye of Rana, and none had the courage to openly disobey.

Prince Polly Tartakower, now a common frog in a tyrannical pond, was initiated into the inner circles of the antiestablishment within weeks of his arrival, by a surly old academic named Makogonov.

"You won't find me writing papers", spat the old codger with a sour wince, "The few of these that read haven't the spine for action. I've seen thousands popped like balloons under Rana's foot, both my parents, seven siblings, several girlfriends, and a cloud of eggs of my own before they even had the chance to hatch! It's an effective deterrent. Our lives are miserable, our suffering is severe and unnecessary. But Rana knows he can maintain order. If he can do that, then he can take and do what he likes. His henchfrogs are very much the same. You will never succeed in upending a ruler like that. Not from within the pond."

Polly puzzled his predicament. He, too, sought to break the people to his will. Makogonov was reassuring, in a way, that such was possible. But looking at Rana upon his mount, Polly was disgusted at the pitiful life the frogs must lead under such a ruler. What was it that made life worth living? And would he choose to deprive others of that very thing to achieve economic goals? Weren't those economic goals going to bring happiness to the people? But there could be no happiness when authority is enforced in this way. Polly could not puzzle his way out.

While much of the intellectual chatter was high falutin, and enjoyed complicating simple ideas, there were some of sound mind and proposition. Makogonov was sandpaper by nature, intentionally provocative, and misanfrogic to boot. While not entirely ingratiating, Igor was certainly less poisonous to one's mood.

"Agency. The individual must perceive agency in himself. The ability to act and better his position. Give him that opportunity. The road maps must be clear, orderly, timely, and accessible. With achievable goals, not too distantly placed, and the encouragement and support of the state, you will maximize, amazingly, both productive participation, and life satisfaction."

Igor was a gem.

"Perhaps a benevolent dictator would be best. All could adore him, he would rule wisely and well, the people could be happy and proud of him as the centre of their collective cultural unity. If we were of better mettle the next and the next would serve capably in that role of virtuous authority. But we know frogs too well. So instead we must find consensus."

"Yes, it's slow. And imperfect. Must it always harbour tension? Is that tension inevitably fatal? Are all states doomed to fail? Is there a great universal rule of life? Can we learn from our histories? Are there patterns and laws to be discovered? Some governing principle? Can we one day shine a light of intelligence to illuminate the dreaded blackness of the future? Is peril advantageous if overcome?"

Sometimes Igor was a gem. He would become ensnared in the immensity of the unknown, wandering for hours in the darkness before finding solid ground once again. Polly would wander faithfully at his side for these happy hours.

Way down the road, not so very far off, a jay bird died of a whooping cough. Well, he whooped so hard, and he whooped so long, that he whooped his head and his tail right off.

"Mummy, that's disgusting! Tell the maid to take it away this instant! You there! Take that away right now."

The maid, Tess, mothered this child for the first four years of her life, but Alara hadn't bothered to know her name. Tess bowed her head, lifted her skirt, and scurried off to dispose of the horrific mess made by this poor bird.

Alara could be said to be the world's greatest evil. Some entitled little shit with no respect for the immense wealth and power of their position. Nobles of old were granted their fiefdoms at the pleasure of the king, and thus required to provide tax collection and soldiery in times of war. The nobles were stewards of the land, maintaining tradition and integrity, to the extent their abilities allowed. With wealth came responsibility. But how sadly social harmony has collapsed, as the rich reign irresponsibly .

The bird wasn't sick. Tess had told Alara so to relieve her of the horror of the truth. That bird had been shot for sport by Alara's father only moments before. The party of three heard the report, and knew of the master's proclivities. Shooting birds from the roof was among these.

The shot that took the head off our poor jay bird was a one in a million. Grand Pooba Kerem won the bet and collected his money immediately from the briefcase of his compatriot, Lesser Pooba Mirac, in an tributary solicitation to gain favour with the Grand Pooba. Knowing both Kerem's vanity and his excellent marksmanship, Mirac had bet that Kerem could not kill that sick jay bird with one shot. Mirac proceeded to supply his friend with a solid gold bullet. One shot, for sport, for a million. Off popped the top, to Alara's disgust. And thus begins our adventure.

"Maid! You take mother along back to the manor. I'll be along in a moment." Alara frequently expressed herself in command. Her every thought beckoned action somewhere, from someone. Mother and maid made off, and Alara walked the spacious forest path out to the edge of the Red Pond, named in honour of the bloody frog carnage often found thereabouts. The pond was avoided as a cursed place. Alara thought that silly, and round about the edge of the pond she walked in a leisurely stroll, thinking herself wonderful, unlike the ignorant ninny goats she must suffer, when what did she spy 'pon the mount in the eye but a shiny gold ball did there lie!

"You there!" Prince Polly was taken aback. But having become accustomed somewhat to his lower standing in the social hierarchy, our proud Prince bowed and scraped belly, in his froggy way, up to this demanding titan, and asked if he could be of service. "Fetch me that gold marble there out on the mount. Try not to touch it too much, you filthy lech."

"Pardon me, princess. But that is King Rana's trophy, his most prized possession, a symbol of his power over the others. The frogs would vie with one another to hand Rana my sorry head. The risk is too great."

"Don't lecture me about some fat froggy king. Get that treasure right now or I'll pull you inside out!" Polly took several cautious hops backwards into the pond, keeping his eyes above the water line, and shivering in a healthy fear.

The impertinence of this blasted frog! Alara was vexed. This beggardly bastard was squeezing her into negotiation. Seeing herself tied down over the barrel, Alara, loathe though she was to do it, considered the compromises she might make in order to acquire her prize.

"Look here you! You go fast and get me that gold. That fat blob won't catch you. Race his little thug army back here with my ball, and I'll protect you."

"Princess, if I have your solemn oath, on your very honour that you will carry me back to the manor and care for me until my dying day, then I will be your champion."

Alara quite liked this chivalrous amphibian. He showed spine, and spirit. "We have an accord, my froggy friend."

Polly turned and stretched into a swim towards the base of the mud mount rising from the eye of the pond, where Rana perched in the pride of his magnificence. Blending into a tribal chant dance in the accepted clockwise manner, Polly surreptitiously began a slow ascent towards the peak. Within a few hops now from the prize, the golden bullet poised protectively under Rana's fanning forefoot, Polly made a maddened dash , and, in an audacious and suicidal surprise, pushed the ball into a roll.. Pandemonium and panic struck throughout the pond, frogs were pounded into submission mercilessly many meters from the mount without rhyme or reason. Most everywhere frogs hopped and croaked, desperate to escape the suffocating mob. Several of the thug soldiers had caught sight of Polly moving suspiciously yonder, half submerged in murky mystery. All frogs in motion, Polly made way almost to the edge of the pond now, and finally one last hop into Alara's billowed skirt, awaiting her prize.

"Wonderful! You are my treasure!" Alara stroked the frog, not thinking him so slimy now, as her champion. The front pocket to her skirt was safe harbour for Prince Polly, as Alara skipped homeward, delighted with the turn of events. Polly croaked happily at his change of fortune. What a match we have made!

Nurses and maids and tutors, gardeners and gate men and guards, the ballet, the opera, the theatre, frivolous foreign fantasies, the heart's deepest waters are stirred. A priviledged Princess and a spoilt selfish frog Prince schemed patricide, and the unification of their houses in marriage. The Prince's pregnant political philosophy would progenate a utopian empire, Polly as the worshipped patriarch. But that damnded Nuck!

Hedges and lawns broke nature's advance. Alara hurried now into the domed palace to the rings of the dinner bells. Into the dining room she did go with imprudent haste, startling the attention of all present. "A miracle has occurred!", she sang suspensefully, hopping three steps to Karem, and producing her beloved in the cup of her hands.

Grand Pooba Karem the magnificent, exalted Magnate Supreme, poked his head forward in shock, his eyes bulged and boggled, his lips ripped bare from the teeth, and he swung a left with panicked ferocity, smacking the cupped hands of his darling daughter. Prince Polly Tartakower, heir to an empire, fired at the wall and, in a burst of spectacular sensation, transmogrified into his naked human self.

"It's that blasted magic forest! Trolls and goblins and sprites and fairies and pixies and leprechauns and the evil of Nuck herself have worried us since time began. And now this naked frog boy!"

"Prince, I will have it known." Polly corrected his posture with pride. And dignity, I'll add. If you have been transmogrified naked you need feel no shame. Be you, and be well. But keep that thing away from me nonetheless.

Grand Pooba could see this lad was resolute, stiff as a rock, and meant what he said. Decisions such as these are puzzling for Poobas everywhere. To this Pooba the problem was thus: I can kill this man, or I can not. The Grand Pooba was suffering through the emotions attached to every possible outcome from the decision before him, when suddenly, from within the frog pocket of her frock, Princess Alara withdrew the golden bullet recovered from the pond by Prince Polly Tartakower.

An alliance was sworn to. Polly would proceed to punish and enslave yet untold millions, uninterrupted, undettered, unyielding for eternity.

HELL'S PRESS

In prison does a man reside, restricted all his days. He'll feed and groom the meat he's in in countless futile ways. He'll tend to psychological distress impossible to phrase. When needs are met, he stops to think, but just gets lost within the haze. The thoughts are all disordered, changing, growing, anaphase. Life, he says, is just some never ending Cretan maze. Collapse, he does, into a torpid, sad, life long malaise.

Preface

Tyranny reigns where we let it. Men are but monsters if permit. Power, you'll see, if you listen to me, obeys an unusual gravity. It concentrates now in the hands of a few, and though it's not solid, it's nothing you touch, the sun it has blotted, as the few they do clutch to the power they hold and abuse. You submit to their ruse. Stitched in a fabric you're knit up in knots, your freedom surrendered to the latest despot. Chained to your place in a prison called nation, the monster on top compels adoration, and if you rebel, I needn't you tell, you'll suffer a freedom castration.

Disobey? This is not something that we can discuss. If you do you'll be branded unfit, treasonous. The wheels of that power will roll over us. If not dead, then your lucky, considered a plus, but you'll not do so again, broken and beaten, a bruised, battered brain, and if you recover they'll open your veins. The power will cower you thus. It's enough to make me cuss.

BILLY GOATS GRUFF

There is much wrong in the world. It is often that when a man dies, the best is said of him, and rarely is this contradicted. But the truth must be faced. Our forefathers, frequently reverenced for their accomplishments, have clearly sacrificed our future for their present. A sorry, selfish lot, our struggles are rooted in their failings. And just who do you think will take responsibility and clean up the mess? You read the news every day, waiting for the second coming, a saviour to relieve you of your burden, and she will never come.

That's rude, of course. You, after all, are a reader, trying to better yourself through knowledge and philosophy. There is hope for you yet. Sadly, your hopes are to be frustrated in the coming pages, for there is little within from which you may profit. Worse yet, you are wasting productive time. When you put the book down, the world will be much as it was when you picked it up.

But don't lose heart! That's just what you're here for. Have a good read, then clean it up. To practice what is so often preached, we must be a century of janitors. Get the place ship shape, raise our kids very well, and the future will be able to take care of itself.

There were three, as there so seldom are. All boys, and all named after their father, William Gruff. On the birth certificate, the names were duly recorded William, according to the wishes of the father. The mother was not consulted, and knew to keep her peace in such matters, as goats had not yet established social institutions to protect the meek from the will of the strong. Were she to disagree, the name would remain William, and she would get a good butt in the belly to boot.

One infant William, the youngest, nuzzled greedily his mother's udders, and mother inadvertently bleated a 'bo!'. The two other Williams had, for some reason or other, picked up on this vocal cue, and bleated it on loop as young Bo stood and looked back and forth between them, naked but for the name.

Willam Sr., and the mother too, adopted this moniker, calling his brothers 'the other two' for about a season before deciding they should be distinguished from one another by appellative. The eldest became Bill, and number two settled for Billy.

At a year's end much has changed for the now adolescent goat brothers. If Bo went for mother's udders, he'd get a hoof, and mother would cry. He thought himself too adult for that anyway, and would disdain interest were he offered. Bo was all enthusiasm for goat excursions with his two brothers. They bullied him, but he was resilient. He surfed a wave of optimistic energy, carving hell bent for leather through all emotional currents.

They'd shaved his hindquarters two months ago, and you could still tell. Bo was ashamed, and harboured a simmering resentment, especially towards Billy, as he had done the cutting. Bill encouraged, and Bo's heart was broken. Billy was sorry he had shaved Bo's ass. It was hilarious at the time, but things hadn't felt right between the two of them since then. Billy missed the bond they had shared before the ass shaving. It felt that this fundamental fracture would haunt their relationship to the crypt and beyond.

Billy was introspective and quiet, and the shaving was unusual. Are things like this out of body experiences? Billy felt like another person had done this. Now the bag was at his feet. Billy learned regret was a slow acting poison, and resolved against actions that would sow the seeds in future.He wasn't a coward though. Bill had tried his level best to break Billy to his will. Bill had imprisoned Billy in their pen while he and Bo went on excursions for three weeks in July. Bill wanted to force sole control of decision making for the group. In the end, Billy neither acquiesced to Bill's demands nor acknowledged Bill's supremacy. He was free. Billy did not regret any of his actions but the shaving, and did not begrudge Bill's attempt. The day he was freed, he was as affable and agreeable as a brother could be, unchanged by Bill's coercion.

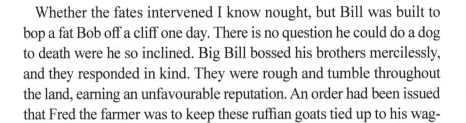

Whether the fates intervened I know nought, but Bill was built to bop a fat Bob off a cliff one day. There is no question he could do a dog to death were he so inclined. Big Bill bossed his brothers mercilessly, and they responded in kind. They were rough and tumble throughout the land, earning an unfavourable reputation. An order had been issued that Fred the farmer was to keep these ruffian goats tied up to his wagon if he was ever to bring them beyond the confines of his farm.

What could Fred do? He never willingly took the three brothers anywhere. He feared Bill like the devil himself. He had stopped mending fences for some time past, as Bill could barge right through anything but a stone wall. The brothers went where they chose. But they steered clear of inhabited areas anyway, after a warning shot once scathed Bill's left horn.

Click. I've snapped by fingers. And I'll draw your attention away to a village quite remote, by goat excursion standards, which at this very moment you are underestimating. This village is remarkable for its predictability. The harvest was steady year after year, the old were replaced by the young in their duties, the tax collection totals never changed, and there was very little to do for the poor official sent to govern this and many other villages like it all on his lonesome.

Bob, for that is what he is called, was a law graduate from the state college whose can-do attitude impressed a few with party connections and had him on the fast path to this glorious outpost, a bit out of the way. A can-do attitude can be a bit much. Bob was of an entrepreneurial spirit, and didn't sit idly by and let his employment under the government dollar go to waste. One year he decided to enforce an environmental damage clause, written obscurely and interpreted loosely by our enterprising official.

Methane emissions were to be controlled within described limits, and not to greatly fluctuate in value. Bob found a finable offence, and thought that was just fine. He drew up charts and was going to inspect homes for their methane output. Month to month he would record, and fine, against great fluctuation in production. It worked, he fined a few people. Most just paid. The fine was so small that they'd rather pay than tackle this ambitious official head on. All the farmers lied on their taxes anyway, and were occasionally shot subsidies they didn't appeal for or expect from time to time. Bob's minor harassments were operational cost. They called him shit-smeller Bob. Or the Troll, sometimes, too.

Bob wasn't really trying to squeeze anybody. Just to let them know that they were under the watchful supervision of diligent officers of the court. And just because they provided a core value to society while enjoying none of its benefits, they were subject to the full interpretation of the law at all times. He intentionally made the fines nominal. And he recorded and submitted with documentation every cent he collected from the villages he administered. Those back home knew Bob was a rising star.

Among other short term enforcement drives to control undesirable activity, Bob took a post controlling banned substance transfer through his administrative region. Puffed with official pride, and the proclaimed authority to exercise the law, Bob set up an umbrella and a chair on a solid stone-lock packhorse bridge, one of several trade access points to his purview, intent on collecting fare for undeclared substance transportation. As it turned out, the heat of the sun was too much for Bob to endure, even with an umbrella, and he accordingly moved his post beneath the bridge, in the shade. He could patrol well enough from here.

He wasn't set still for all that long. Down the crystal path of time clip clopped the billy goats Gruff, sure as drink and the Irish. The sounds of destiny rang in Bob's ears, to the rhythm of a mini goat parade. That's what the future is, a parade, a current, in which we are thrust along, swept perpetually towards an inevitable destiny - a cold wood box in the earth.

Bob had to shake his head. Those clip clops drove him mad. He scrambled hands and knees up the grassy embankment, soiling himself all over, stumbled at the next to last step and landed flat, belly and face scraping across a lightly gravelled path. Up Bob hopped with a grunt, stood scarecrow, straight-armed an open palm and barked, "Stop! By order of authority!" at these three surprised, suspicious travellers.

The Gruff brothers, for it is they, stopped several steps shy, and there they sat. Bob could not overhear their conversation, but they appeared to behold this impudent man and his impudent presumptions according to their characters, and not as one. There is leeway in the goat social behaviour for much disagreement, and they are forever butting heads over their differences of opinion. Goats are capable of identifying both as the individual and the group simultaneously.

After some minutes deliberation, Bo clip clopped confidently towards the bridge and the beast.

"Why are your brothers hanging back there? You go back and tell them to come forward too. This is an inspection of the state, administered by the village cooperative, district 13, farmlands equability oversight council, who have appointed me acting deputy vice secretary for zones 17 through 24. I am therefore requesting that you unpack all of your belongings, fill out this provisional form stating what they are, and then I want a detailed explanation including, but not limited to, your last point of departure, your business in this district, how long you might be staying, any contact information for people you know and for your expected residences here, an itinerary of your dealings, and if you could just fill out forms A23B and AB23-D, recording all this information, then I'm sure we can get you on your way before the moon waxes full. Oh, and those horns are restricted trade articles. I can let you pass, but it's a small fine."

Bo took a long look back at his two brothers, watching expectantly from their chosen posts, quite close together. He turned back, and addressed the toll troll innocently, "That's fine by me sir. Baaa. Of course, I'm not the one carrying currency. You'll have to take that up with my brothers. They'll be right along."

"Did those two shave your ass, little fella?"

"Yes, they did sir, the middle one, my brother Billy."

"You run along. Your brothers can deal with this." Bob had a heart, when he thought he could afford it. And now, he knew, he could really show it.

"I'll sit right down on the far side of the bridge, sir, amongst the luscious dewy tall grass, and fill out these forms for my brothers. You can worry about your fine."

Right, good little fellow thought Bob, as Billy belaboured his steps towards the might of officialdom.

"Son, did you shave that boy's ass? Now, you know that's not right. The damage you can do, not just to another person, and that's an enormous weight, but also the harm you can do to yourself. That regret for an action like that can shape you, disfigure you psycholigically, preventing you from experiencing emotional fulfilment. You'll hate each other forever after for representing this failing in one another. Shame on you! I wish I could arrest you right here and throw you in a cell with men of low standards. Now you run along with your brother and think of how you can atone for your actions." Bob sucked and blew a deep, satisfied, sigh of pure erotic bliss.

Billy dragged his relenting hooves clop by clop across the stonework bridge. Billy sat down to watch with his brother, the paperwork starting to blow away in the breeze. And here Billy, not having to say a word through the whole story, departs with nothing but sorrow and shame and the deepest regret. Later in life, when the legend of their story had spread, a fierce quarrel broke out pitting Bill and Bo against Billy, as their tale was being marketed as the Billy Goats Gruff. The proceeds were indeed split evenly, but Bo and Bill weren't as easy to monetize as celebrities. Billy was taking home a bigger portion of the bacon and his brothers wanted in. Greed, as usual, that's what you might think. But there was a deeper issue. Goat society was, in fact, egalitarian for the most part, and maybe Billy's brothers had a point. Bill walked up with the calm self assurance of the physically superior.

"Sir, there's a fine on those horns."

"I'm not paying."

"Then I'm afraid I can't allow you to cross this bridge."

"You weren't here a week ago. I crossed freely."

"I'm here now, enforcing legal code."

"I do not recognize your authority in this matter. The bridge is free for me to use, and I will use it." Bill is the hero of this story. Bill.

For one painted moment, two brother goats lay in an open slanting field of luscious long grass in the distance, unconcerned as they watched the outcome of an eternally repeating conflict. Tyranny faces off against Freedom in the foreground, in the form of man and goat, before a stone-work bridge crossing a running creek to the land of milk and honey on this occasion. And on this occasion, freedom prevails from sheer strength.

Bill braced his hoofs, lowered the bone battering ram of his skull, skipped forward in a practiced lunge, his entire mass in motion, and crushed flush into Bob's surprised pelvis, lifting him off his feet and propelling Bob airborne over the side off the stonework bridge and out into the middle of the rushing creek, crushing tyranny to death on the rocks below. It took a few more stomps by all three goats, as Bob wasn't quite dead yet. But the goats Gruff managed, for a seemingly rare success by freedom in the modern world.

The gong of fabled lore has sounded for these billy goats. Their triumph over the imposition of the powerful echoes for eternity through these very pages.

HANSEL
AND GRETEL

"It's nonsense."

"It might be. We've all heard the stories since we were kids."

"She'd be long dead. Berries will only get you so many years. God knows what she did to get through the winters."

"Well, as you can see.."

It was a cat. It used to be. Splayed out now, on it's back, like a snow angel. But the snow had melted. The fur looked stiff, like an old leather shoe would look if it had spent a wet winter on the path. Not that any of us would dare touch it to confirm.

"Could've been a dog."

We knew it wasn't a dog.

"I'm not staying" , and if the stiff ground protested, it did so in silence as her rapid maddened gait carried her back down the narrow winding trail under her creased white brow.

"That's the right thing to do" , and another disappeared.

"We're alone."

"No we're not." The slanted smile dispersed some of the tension in the air.

"It's just a cat."

They knew it wasn't. Just a cat. She had stooped at the first tufts of fur on the path a few steps before, behind the bend. He had followed the crumbs methodically, but she had stepped around and found it first. He had had an inner panic at her startled shudder, but with will had not let on. They approached together, quite close, touching shoulders, almost cheeks.

The others were gone now. The mystery was theirs alone. They hadn't moved in a minute. Dangerous to have your focus so absorbed. The belly ripped open, the insides gone but for bits of spine. The skin on the face torn too, the skull crushed. Maybe a sturdy boot could crush a cat's face like that.

Finally the spell was broken and they looked around. Like it might still be there.

"This has been here a while. The skin is stiff."

But it didn't help. The eyes were there. They were seen. Watched, even. Their fear was feeding something. Something in the very air. How could it be so still?

"Do we turn back?"

A moment passed.

"Do we turn back?"

"No." But he meant yes. And now her will was equal to his own. She walked on. He had no choice but to follow.

The trail was a loop. It passed by a lake. They had seen so on the map. The map on the board. At the beginning of the trail. And now the cat was gone behind them. It was a door. They had walked through. And they knew it.

The sky was overcast. But they both noticed it had gotten darker. The bark of the trees, the ridges had a contrast now, veins of black crawling up and down, hiding, what they couldn't tell. And they were everywhere. Like the watching.

Their teeth were touching, tops and bottoms, clenched, foreheads pushing forward. Their steps were fast, but forced. And it went on for a while.

"There's the lake ahead!" A welcome call, said like he'd been saved. They closed the distance in an instant, found a fallen log, and settled down. He feigned a comfort that wasn't felt. She didn't. Her regret was worse than his. She had walked on first. And the door had shut.

They gazed out on the lake, the water still as glass.

"The water's still as glass." , her eyebrows raised, said with joy, and full of hope.

"Glass moves. It's not a solid, it's a liquid."

Her eyebrows fell, her cheeks aswell.

"Let's get going" , and they did.

The steps made little sound, but their attention made them loud. And the watching growing worse with every minute on the path.

"Are we on the path?"

"Yes." But no. They weren't. There was no path. She followed anyway and had no more to say. But then he stopped.

"No."

She looked at him with hate. But what was that above his head? A line of smoke was curling up and disappearing in the cloud.

"Look!" He turned and did. She lead the way again, determined, but for what she couldn't say. The smoke was from a chimney, lost among the trees. It drew up quickly, so it seemed, but when he glanced the lake was gone.

"I"ll just knock upon the door."

"No, don't." But she was gone.

"Come in!" The smile was reassuring, but the gesture left them cold. And worried. And anxious. But now they were in.

An atmosphere, for sure, signifying nothing well. He sat upon the sofa, she wandered over to the fire. Soon a book between her hands was open, but she couldn't read a word. Candles for dim light, and burning wood to keep it warm.

"It's been long since someone's come. I'm lonely all the time."

"We must be going." And they were.

"She must be standing by the fire" thought they both, but didn't share. The light was fading into evening, it was darker than before. Blackbirds hopped among the branches, tree roots slithered through the soil. They walked for half an hour, finding nothing but despair. And it was feeding something hiding, something poisoning the air.

Again the smoke was curling in the distance, disappearing in the air. They thought they stopped, but didn't, and were once again before the door.

"Come in!"

There they were again, the fire glowing, panic sowing, something growing, and then a thump upon the floor.

She peeled it from her boot, her teeth were showing, it was dead. She shuffled through the room, the tension growing, their reluctance left unsaid. A smile again, a mask, something sinister was fed. The kill was added to the cauldron, boil and bubble, toil and trouble, swinging gently in the flames. An odor, it's sour, an gentle soporific. The effects are horrific. He slumps as he sits on the sofa. The flames flicker fire on her face.

Stir the pot, open a drawer, what are those markings drawn on the floor? Something's not right in this gingerbread house, fairie tale perfect, from a book for a child. Curves and not corners, a nook for a mouse, the air is all soupy, a drug, but just mild. A cat, and she's black, they watch her tail sway. The fire, still it flickers, the setting cliché. Quiet, now, calm. The mind drifts away.

Gretel awakes, her wet drool on the floor. She rolls herself over, but can't do much more. She props herself up. Just what time isn't sure. Where's Hansel? By gods! In a cage by the door, unconscious but living, judged by his snore.

"Girl!" she hears, but in a fog, imperious, though quiet, harsh and merry, mean and bright. The black robed witch was hunched and grinning, boney fingers reaching Gretel's feet. Gretel shudders, and seizes with fright. "There is the boy!" witch hisses and waves. "There he is now and there he will stay. Die, that boy will if you run away. Cook him, I will, on that very day."

Gretel was free, alone she could choose what to do with that freedom, to put it to use. Our Gretel was torn, she just couldn't decide to flee from the coop or to calmly abide. The lock on the cage was impossibly strong. To try to walk out of the woods is all wrong. They tried that before, but got lost in the haze. They were trapped in the witch's illusory maze. Dreams of escape filled the first few hut days.

Routine settles in, the terror abates. Hansel and Gretel continue debate about the witch and her purpose, her ultimate plan. They knew very little of this boogeyman. The witch came and she went, if she slept they'd not seen. In a rage she would vent, filled with venom and spleen as she'd reach and grab Hansel, stuck in his box. She'd shake his cage madly, and rattle the lock. Then she'd rush out, shut the door with a slam, What's that about? I haven't a damn.

It wasn't so long before the couple caught on, as Hansel was fed like a pig. But Gretel would starve three days in a row before she was offered a fig, half eaten, with slobber and teeth marks, a hole that a worm might dig. The witch cooked a stew, day after day, a hanging pot over the flames, with dead birds and rats that the vultures deign touch for the burden of a terrible shame. Hansel, they guess, is due for the stew, a meal for Nuck's black hearted dame.

Hansel, he whimpers most of the time. He sleeps when he can, but he's covered in grime and filth and a stench that pervades. The whole of the hut smells of death and decay. He's trapped and he's helpless in the course that's been laid by a cold, unfathomable fate. All he can do from within his cage is moan and whimper and wait. He's dirty, unstable, covered in sores, his back, knees and shoulders do ache. Is it days? Is it hours? How long does he have? Not long till his sanity breaks.

There's many an issue, whether red or dark blue, or it's blue or it's gold, but we're forced to choose. Pick a side, grab an axe and do battle to the death. And all through the fight don't stop for a breath. Keep hammering away with the opinion you hold. Don't shrink from their onslaught. Be stubborn, be bold. Isn't that silly? As if to win is the aim. What is it you win in this childish game? Gather facts, gather evidence, and lay them all out. We'll look them all over with a healthy dose of doubt. We'll struggle with conclusions, and even then we're not done, no opinion ever truly formed, though the proof may weigh a ton. For every time we close that door, we've made a great mistake. "Your work is done, now stake your claim!" promises the snake. First of all the future holds some cards, you will agree. Calculations we will solve will change how things we see. Moreover, once we have seen fit to banish parity, and into law we do commit a present policy, you have become an oppressor, and create an oppressee.

Commandments etched in solid rock, to lead us for all time? These laws you write are hubris, the fundamental crime. You think you know what's best for us? You'll tell us how to live? Directions for our future men you see fit to give? We are born free! And so we should be. What laws we follow, what rules we make, must be left to us. To Jim and Mark and Mike and Dave, to Lucy, Alice and June, too, if she behaves. To those nearby we must entrust the broad interpretation and administration of laws which they are free to adjust.

Write a constitution, broad in theme, to be a guiding light. Basic principles enshrined, our inalienable rights. And then you must release control, and let the people live. Fulfill the promises of freedom that you so easily give. Let his neighbor judge the man that thinks to do him wrong. It's not for the State to tyrannically dictate that he be punished and for how long. Work out in the community what acts are not ok. Each one will be aptly handled. There may be a stray, but, even under strict controls, that happens anyway. The conditions that will lead to crime must be studied well. Alleviate the strain on man, remove him from his shell and let him shine. He has a bed, the man's been fed, the dignity of law, and watch and see what he makes of he once the hunger thaws. Trust in man to do his part if he's treated with respect. Crime is born of suffering and life long felt neglect.

Provide a basic income, food, and medicine when sick. Education, free, accessible, and that should do the trick.

Where were we when we left them? The boy was in the cage. Gretel's mind is split asunder, green stick twisted, splintered. Some days she'd work away at the witches small demands, washing, cooking, cleaning, killing chickens with her hands. Some days weren't so easy, and Gretel would rebel, refuse to do her work, and the witch would beat her well. Some days she'd try to run away, leaving Hansel to his fate. But she'd soon return in circles, the witchy fog would not abate. Is it possible that when we're pushed our character evolves? Gretel one day wakens with an most unshakable resolve. She's determined she will kill that witch, it's high time she should die. What of murder's moral hitch? Please. She deserves it, you know why. The world's better off without her kind. That you will not deny.

The witch is rarely absent more than a day or two. Opportunity there was just to beat her black and blue. But Gretel always found a reason, she would hesitate. The lighting's wrong, the wind is up, and she would have to wait.

The witch, one day, is muttering, a thing she's prone to do. "He must be plenty plump by now. It's time for fatty stew." To the cage she walks. She crouches low and a long arm reaches in. "He's nought but skin and bone, the brat! How is it that he's thin? Not eating what I give you boy? Well I don't care a fig. You'd be going in the stew were your limbs not more than twigs."

Helpless Hansel helped himself, the tricky, cunning boy. He'd kept some bones from supper to serve him as a toy. When the witch grabbed for his arm, Hansel snatched a bone. He let her pinch and yelped in pain, pretending it was his own. Alas! A witch is evil bad, and not a fairie tale. Hansel's ruse just made her mad, the boy was born to fail. She turned away and grabbed a broom, leaving Hansel in his jail.

The witch is hot. She swings at Gretel, just missing with her shot. "Stoke the fire, add some logs, I want the fires of hell be brought! Get up, you scamp, and get to work, you worthless nanny goat. If you don't get that fire roaring, I'll slit your pretty throat."

Gretel's left to tend the fire, the witch prepares the feast. She's chopping onions, carrots too, to accompany the beast. The witch has filled the cauldron with a dozen other things. Iridescent beetles, toad toes, gnats and a sparrow's wing. Scrapings from her fingernails into the pot she flings. A canary from its prison went, when it refused to sing. Thyme and garlic, nettles too, something lucky picked off her shoe, she threw in some star anise, more than a few, and the recipe completed with some ear wax, dug out brand new.

Gretel was sulking down by the fire, staring into nothingness, her situation dire. Arms by sides, her mind it hides, Gretel is forlorn. To die like this, in a witches hut, for this was Gretel born? "Stoke the fire, you damned fool girl!" Witch scampers like a squirrel across the room and grabs the poker from the stand. Cast iron heavy, she prods about, with a stiff, well practiced hand amid the logs, and reveals the coals burning hot beneath. Thinking of the boiling child, a cackling witch bares her rotten teeth.

Gretel feels a surge within, a push to save her mortal skin, an fierce, insistent, ancestral command, an chemical release from some triggered lymph gland. She lunges her shoulder with the whole of her might and knocks the witch headlong, oh, what a sight!, right into coals that are glowing and bright, coals that are snapping with jaws of delight, an miraculous triumph for the good and the right. "Burn, witch! You die!" good Gretel does cry. "Burn the black mage!" Hansel yells from his cage. But where is the key that fits Hansel's lock? It's tucked up somewhere in that witch's black frock!

"Fish out the key from her clothes, Gretel, please! It's been weeks I've been in here. I must stretch my knees!"

"Wait Hansel. You're ruining it. Listen to her scream! Enjoy this, her howls and moans. She fulfills my sweetest dreams." Gretel walks over and holds Hansel's hand. Together they allow their relief to expand and they feel quite merry as the witch burns to clay, screaming much less now, as the flesh melts away. Gretel grabs the poker and stabs the withered witch. She's all but dead now anyway, and Gretel hardly gets a twitch from the crumpled dripping mess. Gretel wears a shining smile, a joy she feels no need to hide. Murder though it be, Gretel finds her sense of justice satisfied. She's much relieved of recent stress.

She fishes out poor Hansel's key from in the glowing coals. Key in lock, the cage is open, and out our Hansel rolls. The filth, the smell, the cuts and bruises, clothes all full of holes. But he's alright, he's safe as church, no goblins, sprites or trolls. Wherever life may lead him now, this boy will wear a smile. Nothing much can happen now to match this fairie trial.

Gretel's gained immensely from this spot of jeopardy. Wherever she finds trouble, rogues or cads or boors or knaves, they're perched among the treetops, around corners, deep in caves, she'll forever have the confidence to face it with resolve. In crisis some will panic, but our heroes will evolve. We meet now for the first time our new Gretel, since reborn. Give this flower space to live, and beware, for she's grown thorns.

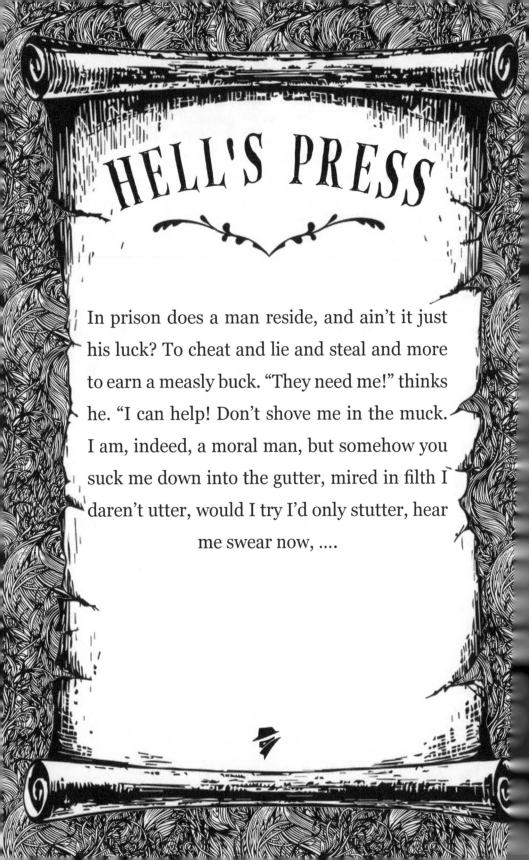

HELL'S PRESS

In prison does a man reside, and ain't it just his luck? To cheat and lie and steal and more to earn a measly buck. "They need me!" thinks he. "I can help! Don't shove me in the muck. I am, indeed, a moral man, but somehow you suck me down into the gutter, mired in filth I daren't utter, would I try I'd only stutter, hear me swear now, ...

Preface

Finally we've reached the end. Nevermore need you expend the energy to read the Tales. But you will, because you must. Fate's winds have blown your ship this far, and one day you can expect another gust. A hand you've on the tiller and you tinker with the jib, your freedom is a falsehood, fate's most favourite flippant fib. The weather keeps you home one night to avoid a fatal crash. You would've won the lottery, but didn't have the cash the week your numbers turned up right, unaware a victim of fate's mischievous spite.

The Piper is the only man who's free of puppet strings, a luxury quite out of reach of earth's most potent kings. That's because he's not a man, but born of fairie blood. His anger can unlock a force of nature like a flood. Worst of all for most of men, he's moral to a fault. Transgress his rules with caution, for he's not above assault. His principles are iron clad, but guess them you cannot. Maybe try a bribe, his acquiescence can be bought. For fairie blood is avaricious, vicious, blunt and cold. The Piper can be blinded by a fair sized pot of gold.

With this advice to guide you, maybe luck will see you through. I hope you've packed a four leaf clover to go with your horseshoe.

THE PIED PIPER

Three Blind Mice

Wren, Sparrow, and Lark, three little field mice run through the park. Who is that having a picnic this day? They can't see at all, so which one's to say? Wren smells fresh bread, and Sparrow the meat. But Lark isn't smelling for a day's tasty treat. This one's not foolish, he's hatched a nice plan, as only at the brink of survival we can. Lark sees a blind mouse won't have half a chance of living a year if he can't find his pants. "Diurnal predators, from dawn to the dusk, will hunt us and kill us with wing, claw and tusk. Then others wake up to stalk in the night. A mouse must be always ready for flight."

Wren's a philosopher and explains it like this, "the body is nothing more than an shell. Ourselves are within, the flesh just a husk. Upon death there is nothing you're likely to miss about living, provided you're not cast down to hell."

"Spurn the moment!" Sparrow sputtered, "How dare you do so! We're here but a blink of fate's fearful eye. We swim in the stream, the strong steady flow of a fluid time sweeps us by. So swim while you can! Backstroke and breaststroke, butterfly, free, in life you're the man!

But you must seize the opportunity! Lay aside your well made plans. Express yourself within the community. Together we'll be us! So much worry, so much fuss eliminated painlessly, wouldn't you have it thus?"

These mice are formidable, intelligent to boot. But they're starving in the park, and must skulk and rob and loot if they hope to live to see the sun in the east rise over head. Like as not we'll find these mice before the dawn are dead.

Sandbox

Rina roamed in innocence to places far and wide, Gita followed faithfully, bolstered to her side. They came across some boys in play around some balls of glass. But they couldn't understand the meaning of a snake eyes or a pass. Rina wandered on across the endless garden lawn, an helpless unwatched simple girl, a pint sized fearless fawn. She comes across a solemn crowd, a stage, an act, a play. The lead says something dark out loud and scares our girl away. On she goes, across the earth, a wide and open path. She shuffles forward to the slide, beyond the fountain bath. Kids play here too, everywhere. For in Hamelin, all the world's a fair.

What a lovely place you've come to while away an hour! The weather's fine, the girls in shape, the bells ring in the tower. All conspire to still your heart in a pixie poisoned way. For never once there was a town, of fabled lore or nought, that lived a life of peace and grace and quarrel seldom sought. For towns are men, and men are towns, and trouble's always found where funds are tight and hungers bite, there's not enough to go around. For now, though, Hamelin's in the black, the money flows in gobs. She's overrun with customers, they're herded through in mobs. Grain they want, all we can grow. We grow it thick as thieves. If it weren't for rotten politicians, administrative sieves, then Hamelin would be fairie perfect, fine in every way. The people woke to yet another fair and pleasant day.

Stowaway

"Lark! What have you done? You've led us to danger, this plan's not so fun." The mice he'd convinced to get into the bag and be carried back home by this porky old hag. At least so they thought, they were blind after all. But they were quite certain by the voice and no balls. Sparrow, that rascal, burrowed that cave. He's shameless and plucky and lucky and brave. The woman got up and collected her stuff, then she paused for a moment, bends over and huffs. The mice in that moment got into the bag, and are now on their way with this horrible hag.

"We'll live with her, hidden." Lark pleaded his case. "A home and a table, a bed and a bath, an endless supply of her grain. All seasons we'll revel in comfort, not suffering under the rain. We'll be warm and fed just like I said, you'll forget what it's like to complain."

Sparrow's unsure and Wren thinks it's crap. They're both afraid they'll be caught in a trap, or killed with some poison, or stuck on some glue. The ways that mice perish are more than a few. Undaunted, unwavering, Lark grits his teeth, but just to be safe he buries beneath all the stuff this gal carries around in the bag. Things will be fine if his brothers don't nag.

Off they go in a cart, to the porch of a home. A man opens the door, he's holding a comb. He's bald, which is puzzling, but not to his wife. She knows something's wrong with this y chromosome. He can be witty and charming, with a wide pleasant smile. But once he has what he wants you'll get nothing but bile. He'll shout and he'll stomp, if you let him he'll tear at your clothes and your papers, maybe even your hair. Say hello to this man, don't short on the pomp, for standing before you is Hamelin's fat mayor.

"I've been called to the office, I'll be home at five. Make dinner for three, serve oysters alive. I'm bringing a girl, next to me she will sit.

She's desperate I sign off on her liquor permit. Be quiet at table, and when you hear me cough, make haste, hurry up, and kindly screw off. You won't like the customs of business like this, for they're traditionally sealed with the gift of a kiss. It's normal, my woman, it's nothing but form. Let's settle this now instead of making a storm in front of the girl. In return I'm gifting her your mother's pearls."

Into the kitchen she heads with a frown. The mice scurry out as she puts the bag down. This is the hard part, they're all in the dark. The two brother's pause, then run after Lark. A tragic undoing, near fatal, mistake. Lark knew no better what direction to take. They all ran after the fat man's wife. She cut off their tales with a carving knife. Have you ever seen such a sight in your life? Three blind mice.

See how they run? Straight out the door in anger and pain. They flee to the forest, but behind leave a stain, a trail of tail blood spilled upon the path, dark and red and menacing, a scent picked up on fast by a pack of three such female rats that never did you see. Horny and aggressive were these dangerous rats. The blind mice all agree. "Revenge we'll seek, for damage done, upon the race of man. And through these horny rats, my brother's we'll show the world we can."

The blind mice mated rats that night, in an act of angry vengeful spite. The progeny forthcoming are a franken-hateful-fear. If you happen to run in to one, I advise you to stay clear. The pack grows ever larger from a group of three or four to a herd of several dozen and from thence come even more. They will eat through all your produce, not for food but from delight at disturbing your existence and in adding to your plight. They hate you, pure and simple, and will haunt each waking hour. But it's worst at night, they'll screw you right by eating through the flour. Grain is Hamelin's commerce, with a premium for grinding at the mill. The rats will gorge themselves, Nuck's power slowly binding.

Piper

There was a girl, her name was Kate, she loved a dwarvish king. Though he wasn't handsome, tall or strong, she couldn't find a thing he wouldn't do for her, and so good Kate said yes. The fates have long been calling Kate, the good they like to bless.

His world was through a tunnel in a mountain in the east. Kate went through and met that world a dozen times at least, often wishing she could bring to us the dwarf civility. The world of man could not adapt, we hadn't the ability to behave with grace and charm and kindness, all with great humility.

Alas! One day the bridge collapsed between our world and theirs. Fate is fond of giving out and taking each its share. You'll never unravel the spin of the marvel of fate's most mysterious affair. Kate was stuck in our world while the king was on his side, obliging to the law, for on his presence they relied. The hole collapsed, and never more did these two lovers meet. But, of consequence, into our world a Prince I'll have you greet.

A child was born to Kate and, in the turbulence of fate, the boy was tall but underweight, and by the age of nine or eight displayed the queerest piebald trait of the most dashing bright array of clothes in which to robe himself most gay. Happy smiling, twirling in the lilies, styling hair on forest animals that came at his request. For this dwarvish giant prince could lull with song. His very tune would quite arrest your heart and mind and seep into the fabric of your soul until you slept in dreamless slumber, swept upon the wave of tune. To the brink of your destruction you are led like a buffoon.

Piper! He has arrived. How have you survived without his sharp, but cheerful wit? But beware his dwarvish anger, do not question his resolve. Your transgressions he won't suffer, misbehaviour not absolve. He'll kill to punish beyond measure, past considered fit. To fate he is a reaper, causing havoc in his wake. A fourth is flat, the tempo lost, and now he's on a break. He alone amongst the men will plot and set his course, liberated from the fields, the fabric of the force, the dimensional lines we can't even imagine, from an unknown unknowable source.

"Mother, dear, you are a saint. I've loved you all my days. You've tried your best to train me to be kind in every way. I am, I'd say, a moral man, by laws I do abide. But when I see injustice done I won't sit on the side. Retribution I will have, revenge I will pursue. Brutal will my vengeance be, not just a slap or two. Dwarvish law prevents the crime from happening again by slaying a genetic line, we want not harmful men. This law I bring to save us from destructive evil cads. If that means slaying children, well, bring on the little lads. I'll kill the instinct to be bad, believe me that I will. For only I have nerve enough to administer this prophylactic pill."

Kate, she sits in silence. Her thoughts are all her own. Piper is her only child, she loves him to the bone, but his penchant for eugenics Kate, in conscience, won't condone. She knows this is a parting from her one and only son. If he is going to murder, then she is forced the boy to shun. On this last day she counsels him of stain he must beware, for acts of evil in our life, our souls we shred and tear. Even with his dwarvish blood, though he may take great care, a life eternal is not his, "Mortality we share, my son. Farewell." Kate will shed many a tear, I fear, even for the souls in hell.

Where Piper wanders for many a year is, I'm afraid, not certain, not entirely clear. A lack of a man, I think I might see, a teller of stories, a man quite like me. He needs imagination to see aardvarks ski. Or to have human hair growing out of a tree. What would it be like to not have our knees? He likes talking fish and exotic disease. It would be best if he weren't so hard to please.

A pipe Piper found one day. Left behind, as some might say, the owner's demise came an unusual way. At home he was found, in no way was he bound, but he'd eaten an chain anyway. The man, a musician, a poor showing had given, drunk as he was. Piper was driven to address the man thus, "Man! That was bad. I'm frightfully mad, I've paid and you cheated, you foul, thieving cad!"

"Bum luck!", said the man, "sometimes I'm ok. Pay again tomorrow, you'll see me play."

At this Piper went to the man directly and took the instrument from him. In a haunting, ghostly, druid voice, the Piper gentle starts, a pair of alternating bass notes slowly climb the octave chart. Somehow the man begins to feel a grip upon his heart. Up he gets and wanders while the Piper plays the tune. There's the chain, he has it now, and now is not too soon, he stuffs the chain into his mouth and swallows, the foolish buffoon. But he hasn't the slightest chance of escaping Piper's trance, lifted from his pants into a will-less flood from Piper, a gift of his dwarvish blood.

And now our Piper has the pipe. It's his, is as just and good. According to his principles, his coin as well he should, and he does, the Piper, take the man for everything he's got. Dwarvish laws are unforgiving, and the Piper's blood has not forgot. If you think the Piper brutal, I implore you stay away. When you listen to his song compelled you are to him obey. None will stop his purpose, none his path will intercede. You will do as he commands, you'll suffocate or bleed. You'll kill your wife and then your child, you'll mix milk in your rum. You won't know where you're going to or where you're coming from.

The piper plays a soulful tune and life just must respond. It's from the dimensions our senses can't see. And that's before knowing our senses deceive. It still is a part of our reality, matter in fields that we just can't perceive. Measure what we can, that's good, but theory must look beyond. It's in the math, our greatest tool. So calculate until you drool! I'll let you stop once you've made a pool.

These other dimensions, beyond comprehension, they rarely take act in our own. Though not impossible, it's not like the gospels, but go on and think on your own. I'm not here to tell you what it is you should think. By god, I'll sure let you put milk in your drink! But for science and its application we should surely pay if we are to utilize our resources in an even and balanced way.

Long has the piper roamed over the land. We find him now somewhat grizzled and tanned by the kiss of the sun and the touch of the wind, he's not quite as spry and his hair slightly thinned. Determined in justice the piper has been, and so it will be to the end of his life, till death steals this dwarf and his ethics fuelled strife. And now you have met, then we're set to continue past valley, in vale, by river, through forest in gulley and dale, to the heart of our legend, our shared fairie tale. Hamelin's in sight for the piper at last, awaiting fate's die by Piper be cast.

The Deal

Hamelin would be fairie perfect, fine in every way. The people woke to yet another fair and pleasant day. But what came next, the whole affair, is rather difficult to say. Shame and horror, guilt and cruelty, morals delicate to weigh. Hamelin's tale is only for the fairie tale gourmet. The rats come in a vengeance, retribution to inveigh.

At first they aren't much noticed. They're seen in ones and twos, caught in kitchen cellars, or crawling over shoes. The people start to talk about the problems that they make. Just what it is that they should do, what precautions they should take. Some are laying poison out, some are grabbing brooms. Cats are hunting everywhere, in each and every room. It's not enough, the rats still spread, determined in their doom. A week goes by, their numbers grow, the stored grain's getting thin. The fields are bare, rats ate it all, no harvest's coming in. Nothing done can stop the rats, and, much to their chagrin, the town concedes against the rats they simply cannot win.

The young are in a panic. Their screaming fills the air. The old are much more stoic, absorbed in silent prayer. Many carry handkerchiefs to mop a teary face. We'll not humiliate them in this very special case, for I would be found sobbing, curled up fetal on the ground if these vicious rats in masses came laid siege within my town. Cupboards barren, money spent, the water's stained and brown. They chew and gnaw and bite and claw, they scratch and make a mess. They're everywhere and all at once, a growth we can't suppress. We're on the brink, we're at wit's end, and now I must confess I'm off to drink one with a friend, I do humbly acquiesce.

Jerome the gnome, mayor of Hamelin, sat fat and official, defended by a broad oak mayoral desk. You've met once before, so you know what's in store from this self serving whore. "You lousy, sub intellect, bleating, furred moo! I'm blaming this whole god damn mess upon you! You were cheap and indulgent, you let them begin, and now they're amok! Tell me, where they're not in!? An election is coming, just a twelve-month to go. You're fired! It's all on you. Get me re-elected. I'll find you something new. Now call in those guys that came in from the zoo."

"You there! You guys go round up these rats. You can use nets, bullets or cats. I don't care what you do and I won't ask you why, but those rats have to go or we're all going to die."

In runs a man with a worried nervous look. In his hand he holds but one sad lonely chewed up tattered book. "It's all that's left! They've come and eaten every single page. Our knowledge, lore and custom gained in struggles over ages gone in days. This infestation must be stopped! Or the mayor's head, off it will be chopped!"

Here comes a girl, a forehead full of furls. So young to be anxious, but she's trying to be brave. "These rats, my lord! Have no respect, they fill each nook and cave within my home and in the street. They cannot decently behave! I've come upon a prayer that the state my soul will save!"

A third shuffles in, this one just a child, "My tummy is empty, I haven't eaten for a while. No grain, one can't get fed. Can one of you here spare some bread?"

"Out, child, now! That's enough of your complaints." He was pushed out the door and later put into restraints.

"You bastards are staining my triumphant campaign! My career is over and my secrets out! My guilt and my shame! No! I'll not have it. We're stopping this game. Set fire to the buildings. We'll burn the place down!", when in pokes the head of a mysterious clown. Or colourful, one might say. "I'm Piper. I can help, if you'll pay."

"You can? And you will? You'll get rid of the rats? At least from the homes of our voting aristocrats? Piper, my hero, a thousand guineas for you if the promise you offer can be made to come true! I don't mind that you dress like a nance, a rainbow of colours all over your pants. Get out there and get them! These rats you must kill. Come see me after and we'll settle the bill."

They shook on the deal, or was it a bet? The fat hand of the mayor was covered in sweat. He'd rent out his wife to be done with this threat. The Piper accepted. It seemed a fair trade. He'd get rid of the rats and then he'd get paid. Should we hold him responsible for the mess that's been made? Posterity records the horrors he brought. Are they balanced out? Was a moral lesson taught? Was retribution worth it? Is the end sum a nought? A question I will leave not for me but for you, a puzzle, a conundrum, in your leisure to undo.

Hero

Piper walks out in the street with a grin. Money made so easy that it ought to be a sin. The musician's pipe he fondles as he raises to his chin the stiff hard wooden barrel, so long loved it's next of kin. On it Piper blows a mournful, slow and haunting air. A tenor voice is carried off to all, a sad compelling prayer. All are in appreciation, most of all the wicked rats. They come running to a siren's song, small, furry acrobats.

Gather in wonder as the Piper he plays, and the rats follow after in a trance or a daze, the tune reminiscent of a lute or a lyre, as if one were accompanying a funereal pyre. Swaying together, in step with the lot, down through the streets at a fair ratty trot, they swarm and they clamber, black, brown and grey, a dense hairy mass, a menacing fray. Into the forest the tune they obey. Tangled and winding, through vales they are led. Past dale over glen, with Piper at the head of a queue stretching back to the edge of the town, a horde of these rats in the steps of our clown.

A lunge and a perry, a feint and a twirl, the Piper plays faster and spins in a whirl. The rats, they grow frantic. They chirp and they hiss. They scream and they cry and they completely fail to notice as they draw closer to a stream. Piper climbs in a boat, pushes off from the shore, away does he float, rats follow in hordes. The music the piper continues to play. The rats in a fury, a blind tense melee climb over each other, a scramble together, a fierce and psychotic sprawl into the water. Rats drown in hundreds and in half an hour the stream is dyed red in the suicide slaughter. The Piper plays softly now, some rats still linger. But somehow the impulse to drown oneself stronger! Finally every last rat meets their maker, or at least his subordinate front man caretaker.

In a boat in a stream in a river dyed in blood stands our Piper, the hero, our worshipped nancy stud. All the rats are dead, and standing on the shore are many varied villagers trying to ignore the Piper's calls for some assistance. He's forgot the bleeding oars. They're under some dead rats right there the Piper tries to say. The villagers just standing there, not one among them wouldn't swear the Piper spoke a foreign tongue. The villagers depart en masse, the Piper's left alone. Piper pops into the stream with all the floating mess and swears they will atone for their discourtesy.

Let us leave the Piper too, and maximize his rage. We can leave him on his own for at very least a page. We'll call him back if much in need, but I doubt we'll want him now. The town erupts in joyous glee. Proclaim defeat over the gods sent pestilence in an raucous intoxicated splendour of gender fluid joy. Let him be her and him do him while she and he and her are three, and more there are than I have seen so who am I to say. You're free to do for you, as is your due to being with the right to choose the use of you and your heredi-tary horn. Ankle, back, or armpit, cheek, whatever freaks your beak, for that you shall surely seek. The people of Hamelin will celebrate the day and we would be remiss were we not to have a little peek.

His mouth, her ass, his hand, I'm feint, the town awakes with much complaint. Let's rest another day or two and forbid discus-sion of our immoral milieu. Can you believe Fred and Annie!? They seemed so nice. Who knew? Can't say about after, but damn that was fun. You wouldn't do that in the bright light of the sun. For all our neighbours' puritanical mores, give them half a chance and they're eager to act as whores. That's best done in the shadow and the dark, anonymous, unfettered, unrestrained, and stark. Did you know the banker is a shameless bottom gay? Or the butcher likes them chubby, or miss teacher likes ass play? The mayor's wife gob-bles like a rooster, much admired as she performed. No surprise before too long a healthy line had formed. We'll keep it just between ourselves, a secret bit of bliss. I'm glad to know within us dwells the passion for a kiss.

A few days slowly pass. Sober enough to see, Hamelin's not a child, observes the cold reality that their position isn't mild. Clean the rooms, and sweep the floor, restore the fences and the door, set wrong right where suits you best, you do for you, might I suggest. And so we should on ourselves rely when Nuck has locked on us her eye. That ancient, evil, toxic witch, blotting colour with her pitch, a fickle fate sews cross-stitch, so harmful yet important which without our experience of love and life would not exist. We can hide from her at times, at others we must run. But face her we must and many times before our time is done. Face her brave and strong and true. Make sure you behave as only you can do, a you that deep inside is well and truly only you.

Hamelin's put to rights as much as could be done. The celebration over for the victory they won. The rats are dead. But through the long cold starving winter can the people and their lives endure? To the mayor the people turn, the fat boy pompous gnome. What has the state prepared for us? You're on the hook, Jerome. At every easy problem solved they like us to applaud. Look how wonderful they are! The populace is awed. But when the Nuck brings darkness to life's game, officials hunt for one to blame. Not me! It's him! We'll string him up and set him straight, we'll end his darkness, you just wait. As long as someone's punished, right or wrong we'll close the book on this discordant song. Officials breathe a sigh of deep relief. A bullet dodged, a fate escaped, a never will thou be my grief. Look again at what I've done! Praise me, praise me! We're I a woman I'd be a nun. And if I am one, the rules still hold, she wants to shine like polished gold.

"Hands up, Hamelin for your mayor, hallelujah, man, I swear you're so lucky that I was there. The rats would've run you all out of town."

"Don't forget about our friend, the clown!"

"I found the right man for the job. Now take a knee, you filthy mob! Listen up, I'll tell it straight. Hamelin's in a tricky state. I said I'd pay that clown a wad, but if I do we'll all die over the winter." Harken back to what I said about the kind of tale you would be fed.

A sudden silence fills the air, a peculiar puzzled presence waits. Eyes cast down admiring footwear, shuffles, coughs, ungainly gaits. "Nuck him!" yells a voice within the room, echoed suddenly, to their doom. "Nuck him!" shouted him and her, "this loss we simply can't incur. Nuck him!" chanted hot and swollen faces, fist pumps, dances, warm embraces. When who should walk in through the door, but our old friend Piper, and he's feeling kind of sore.

"The rats are dead. I've done my bit. Pay me a thousand guineas and we'll be done with it. I warn you I'm not the kind of man to cross. Be grateful for what I've done for you. To betray me will be your loss. Do not act with unconsidered, ill advised caprice. Pay me and I'll move on in peace. "

"Nuck him!" someone mutters, many others make it matter, mouthing "Nuck him!" hot and bothered, and he's bellied out the room. "We cannot fulfill our promise, clown, and compromise ourselves. We'll keep our money and save our skin, you freaky, piebald elf."

Pushed roughly to the street, Piper stumbles on the lawn. An old woman has a broom in hand and chases Piper on. He gets away, she catches up, the gal's chase undeterred. He's round the block three times or more, her fitness is absurd. On one more lap poor granny's finally running out of breath. If she keeps it up much longer this will surely be her death. There's a lesson to be learned from this athletic escapade. Don't just think her old and harmless, pent up anger over decades want be violently repaid. Piper's lean and light and sinewy. He's built for flight and can continue. On he goes for quite a while and finally he's put granny out of sight.

Now he has the pipe. Softly, gently, with great care, the precious pipe he pulls it out, veiny, thick and bare. What will he do, this clownish man? The question's in the air. To his lips the pipe is placed with the grace of the devout. He blows a note, the children twitch while parents' gasp and shout. Then begins in bass note trills, some flourishes, some flattened fifths, some fills, a melody, a gravity is born. Children, children everywhere! They drop their toys, they gawk and stare. And then they follow, closely bound by spell or charm, to the Piper's sound throughout the streets, and by the parks, by every house, and all will join the Piper's arc, a ship for children in a swoon, swept on dwarvish waves, a paralyzing tune.

Rita waltzes, skips and bends, copied faithfully by her friend. They dance to Piper's lilting lead, following merrily, mind and deed. All through Hamelin do they roam, past each and every family home. Every child of every age with light toned eyebrows, as one might gauge, fell into the same unnatural, poisoned daze, trapped inside an inescapable aural maze. They approach the town square in Piper's merciless hypnotic haze. And when Piper suddenly ceased to play, each and every child in Hamelin chose to blissfully obey.

They drop their arms, their chins are down, held by Piper's dwarvish charms. Disregard his nancy gown, the sound is what compels the child to be submissively beguiled. All this while the people filed beside the children on parade, at first bewildered, then concerned, parents huddled sad, afraid. Some try grabbing from the stream their child and tried to stop the dream. Before they've had a breath of thought, the child goes mental once by the parent caught, thrashes, kicks and scrapes and bites and worse yet joined by other vicious little snipes! The parents surrender their hopeless endeavour and must accept failure to our stubborn vigilante, a jurisprudence epicure. The Piper will make the town pay.

In a town courtyard there stands a lean man. He's dressed like a rainbow, he's tall, strong and tanned. He has in his hands a stiff wooden wonder upon which he blows a hypnotic thunder, under the spell of which children do follow. They're standing here now, but they're vacant and hollow. And then comes the vibrating bass from the pipe. The air is electric, the moment is ripe. The Piper, he slithers about on the keys, the children are stirring, increasing degrees. They're turning and spinning, and whirling in place. Faster he plays and the children keep pace. Round and round at a rollicking rate, each child their best can't their appetite sate. Soon they are dripping in pools of their sweat, slipping and falling and twitching, but never capitulating, despite the obvious and terrifying mortal threat. On and on the song flies, as Piper's thirst for dwarvish justice never dies.

Rina's a champ, she's there to the last. Gita held strong, but is fading now, fast. Less than one child in ten's going on with the spin. Gita's done well, but now she gives in. Tripping and stumbling in the circles she makes, drooling, unseeing, a belaboured breathing, and cursed with some violent, spasmodic head shakes, and finally, at last, Gita down she does go. She crumples unconscious, an exhausted little doe. Soon the others follow in Gita's demise, but Rina's going strong, to the Piper's surprise!

Rina's spinning circles like an olympic gymnast vet, while the Piper's getting nervous, he's already drenched in sweat. Every child in Hamelin has succumbed to their fatigue, which lights Rina's accomplishment with all the more intrigue. The Piper knows that some like these can fill the hero's role. And here is one to show us all, this defiant little soul. The Piper lays the pipe aside, with emotional effect. He, too, can be made to feel a pure, profound respect for one of ours who pass his test. The day is hers! He'll let her rest.

Around the town, in crumpled piles far spread, are all the children still as statues, for they were all stone dead. The dwarvish law he has fulfilled with the countless children he has killed. An stern, uncompromising, merciless law to which the Piper clung. Perhaps a flaw, but so much a part of his nature that to set it right would be like a medical procedure that could change his height. In the world of men, he is a lunatic that measures moral transgression with a misshapen yardstick, a code of ethics far from the humane politic. A bloodline dwarvish arithmetic that doomed the Hamelin children for the actions of their parents, in a retribution archangelic. Except for one, who carries on. Not for brains was she preserved, nor beauty, wealth, her parentage or brawn, but determination. A soul of steel has Rina here displayed, her dwarvish debt absolved, and her life deserved.

HELL'S PRESS

In prison does a man reside, but not alone, alas! He tries to get along with all, make way to let them pass. But one can't help to cause some harm in a world that's made of glass. And look here now, the concrete towers encroach upon the grass. Each step a man may wish to make, another will claim trespass. In leisure together, whatever the weather is what we should learn in class. The men who put this place together spent far too much time in mass.

ACKNOWLEDGMENTS

Forefathers

Charles Perrault was French, it's true. Don't let that put you off. "What?" you say with scorn and sneer, a gesticulating scoff, "A Frenchman in acknowledgement? To him your hat you doff?"

Yes, I do, he's quite a man, for Charles I beg a truce. For in the world of Fairie Tales, Charles, you'll find, is Zeus. He was the first, among the best, at taming Mother Goose.

To Anderson I give a nod, a writer best, bar none. Fairie Tales of finest silk this author for us spun. To this man I bend the knee, I owe this man a tonne.

He fell from bed one winter day, and left us with the loss. His blood has inked these pages, and for me he is the boss. If Hans were here to read this book I'd hope he'd not be cross.

The Brother's Grimm are next in line, I'll trumpet out my praise. I owe them, too, they've set the stage, they've never left my gaze. A tribute I will pay to them, they've helped in endless ways.

The Fairie Tales are fluid and they need not be so cute. A moral incubation but denies us their true loot. The brothers set us on the path of most delicious fruit.

Acknowledgment I pay to these and others of their kind, contributions gifted to a warped and twisted mind. The lens through which I've seen them will, I fear, be much maligned.

Outcasts

On any given tree a few of the branches are gnarled and twisted, warped and deformed, demented and how couldn't they be? Branches of our human kind will bear the oddest fruit. Some grow pleasant pigment, and to these we all salute. But some have moral defects, a malady that's most acute. Only few can tell the difference, only those the most astute.

Acknowledgment I owe to those that grew all gnarled before, suffered for their differences, invective on them poured. Some because they're ugly, some because they snore. Some because they're lazy and some because they whore. I'd let them all do as they like, the rules I do abhor. Freedom is my only rule, freedom I adore.

Tribute I will pay to these, the outcast, shunned, eschewed. The men and women not the same the world chose to exclude. Especially the ones that feel themselves by norms subdued. Without them fun would starve to death in a world of servitude.

Push back against the rules they make, don't let yourselves be jailed. Imprisoned, maybe not, but still it's oppression thinly veiled, a moral tyranny forced on us, standards we've inhaled. Every law they pass on us is freedom but curtailed.

Family

Who's up next to get some thanks from quarters it's not want? This soap box is the perfect spot from which my thanks to flaunt.

There's my family over there, looking sick and gaunt. Methinks my thanks, though it's legit, has the sound of a smirking taunt.

I see you ducking from the words, pretending you can't hear, wary of the backhand praise in retributive fear. Don't worry so, we won't name names, you're safe, you're in the clear. My name attached to yours will not your reputation smear.

But thanks I'll give, cause it's deserved, without you I'd be lost. Your influence has pressed on me, on me you are embossed. And though I've often shuddered from your callous, heartless frost, I'm more than willing, to know you more, to suffer any cost.

Acknowledgement I'll give to you, my blood, my family. Admit, though it's not perfect, that we've nurtured quite a tree. The branches splay out all directions in wondrous variety. This thanks is all for you, without you I'd not be me.

I like me quite a lot, although I know quite well you don't. If you'd prefer I'd quiet down, let's be clear, I won't.

Helen

The authors that have led the way, the rebels that rebel. Friends and family have I called out in acknowledgement as well. But one most precious waits within my heart. Her thanks I'll stand and tell.

Once I was a vagrant, traipsing lone across the land, till you caught me on my travels, stopped me, took me by the hand. Now, forever more, your lightest wish is my command. Once I was a fishy, swimming lost in oceans wide. You caught me in your net and magic potion you applied. Now if asked I'd swim in fire, and for you my death abide. Once I was a mongrel without a home, without a place. You came and took a hold of me, and leashed me just in case. Now we are together, and no force can ever part. My days are yours forever, as hand and paw are interlaced.

Helen, you are something that my words cannot define, a magic creature hid amongst us, you're an omen, you're a sign. You have loved and you have tortured, you have changed my blood to wine. You are all, and ever with me, every thought I have is thine.

Hugo

The one and only Hugo is at the core of what I do. He is the rhyme, he is the reason, he is the impetus. The Fairie Tales don't happen if there never was a you.

You came all of a sudden on a dark mid-summer's night. Now dark has been abolished and every eve is bright. The Tales are written for you, they are your birthright.

You are written in the margins, you are here in every scene. You're the heart of every hero, you are every villain's spleen. You are the only critic I want to please with this cuisine.

Wherever life does take you, I will always take your side. Anytime there's danger I will always be your guide. Any malice, any anger, any hate you have inside, for you I will do anything, I always will abide.

Hugo, when I'm dead and gone, or when you've left the nest, there is no need for sorrow on life's merry pointless quest. Every problem can be solved, and every issue be addressed. When death comes to take me, I swear I won't protest, so long as Hugo lives on healthy, happy, I can rest.

Through trials and tribulations, Hugo, never once forget: for you alone I've lived this life and I feel no regret.

Friends

Time enough left on the page for wrongs I must amend. Wait I won't till chance is past and hindsight will append. These I must acknowledge and these I must defend. Where would I be, what would have happened had I not a friend.

The Africans are easy going, not too fussy, lots of fun. I've been lucky with the ones I've met, a lottery I've won. The Europeans are suspicious, at first they're hard to know. But once you're past the gatekeeper, the conversation flows. North Americans have, I'd say, rich personality. I really like that they don't stand on staunch formality. South Asians are a tranquil lot, don't judge by history. Why they're not loved by all the world is quite a mystery. East Asians are a measured bunch, they keep things in their place. The farther east you go, I'd say, the more you'll feel their grace. Once you hit the ocean wide, you'll not find a better race. The ones down under, sound of thunder, out for plunder, pirates in their hearts. Careful you don't get them drunk, they'll show their private parts.

Specifics would be tactless. I'll not fall into that trap. Friends are great, I love them all, we'll consider that a wrap.

COUNT FATHOM

The Tales

Born into a world of sin, a hateful paradigm, I am a man that turned his back upon his place and time. Escape with me in Fairie Tales, or charge me with a crime, but read you will, cause read you must, for reading is sublime. Up through the branches of the tree the faithful souls will climb. Listen well within the tree, enlightened bells do chime. I hear them clearly in my heart, and often they do rhyme.

A journey together, in play not in haste. For hurry we mustn't, for hurry's a waste. The breath and the syllable each have a taste. If you move on too quickly, the meaning's misplaced. Like eating gourmet, but it all tastes like paste.

Savour the words in each story I tell. The book is an organism, each word is a cell. You need the right tools if you want to read well. Patience is one, and irreverence is swell. The sentences house things, not unlike a shell, maybe a meaning or maybe a smell, maybe encouragement for you to rebel. You'll have to look twice before bidding farewell.

One day, I am sure, I will sit on your shelf, all knowing, all seeing, an unruly elf. Perched in my place I will know your true self. And you will know mine.

Irreverence

I hate and I hate and I hate! But it passes in time. And what's left behind? I can't really say. It changes in seconds, it skews day to day. I am what I am at the moment, that's true. Be sure that I'm me when I'm talking to you. But look back in time, pick a day from the blue, what was it you said?, was that man really you?

That's me, your new friend, whose been tickling your ear. Hello, here I am, at the end of the book. A custom so odd, just peculiar and queer. You know me so well, but my hand lies unshook. And now here we are, not too late to appear. What's wrong, might I ask? Your look's so severe.

I get that a lot. It litters my path. My thoughts can incite in some others their wrath. Little Bo Peep just can't keep her legs shut, and Little Red Riding Hood works as a slut. Can't I think so or say so if that's what I like? Would it be more PC if I wrote one a dyke? Lighten up, take it easy, your heat gives me a tan. I'm not anything more or less than a man.

We're flawed, I'm aware. It's not really that bad. The littlest things make you crazy hot mad. I write for enjoyment, both others and me. I quite understand if it's the wrong cup of tea. I hope some will like it, the way that I write. I consider each story quite happy and bright. It brings me great joy to see them this way, strong, fearless, and willful, on a drunken moral sleigh, speeding recklessly downhill in a bout of cheerful play.

Tradition

The inception of a mythos we have buried back in time. Story follows story, and corrupts it line by line. I'm adding fuel upon a pyre to keep a memory lit. Change it does what's come before, but don't say that's a crime. Jack had all but wedding rings. Bo found a man that fit. Red defeated semi-evil and kept a little bit. Goldi traipsed on property and got away scot free. Rumpelstiltzkin's faithful to his type, so don't blame me. Perhaps the miller's daughter isn't what you thought she'd be. But it's just another branch you'll find that's growing on the tree.

Fairie Tales are living, they will last beyond us all. Aesop taught us much with just a tortoise that could crawl. You can bet I've got a Cinderella coming to the ball. Don't expect the whole damn lot, a dozen heard the call. More there are, than I can count, red bricks upon this wall.

Love

Love is a word that defies explanation. Source, if you will, it's effect or causation. Find, you will not, to eternal frustration. But yet it's a word known across every nation. Follows it not any rules of gestation. What is it then? Flirtation? Elation? Why does it suffer such frequent fluctuation? What are the ingredients it needs for creation? It seems not to need any solid foundation, but springs up unaware, like a monstrous mutation. Your heart feels a sudden unexpected palpitation. Will it last? Is it true? Does this love have duration? The answers, while sought, cause a burning vexation. I'll say what I know, not a lot, in ovation. Love is a kind of spiritual dilation.

Love is attached at the hip, for this man, with duty, obligation, to fulfill a demand. It's not just a word, but more like a gland. Love compels action, don't misunderstand. Do, you must, if in love you trust, all that you can, whether moral or not for love is not above a touch of slight of hand. A paralyzed love deserves reprimand. In some places and ways love's considered contraband. But not here. Here in abundance you can find love, in the land of the Fairie Tale.

Growth

Once I was child, in the garden I did play. Satisfaction I would seek and I did not delay. From game to game, from friend to friend, I sought out pleasure til the end, when mother called and home I'd go, backpack dragging, footsteps slow.

I grew much bigger day by day, and change, they did, the games I'd play. But still inside I felt the child, unruly, impatient, proud and wild. How could I attain some pearls? Then, perhaps, I'd catch the girls. I'd scheme and plan and plot and grouse to earn fate's fortune from my stool in the alehouse.

Older still I soon became, by then I'd given up the game of chasing fortune here and there, while tearing daily at my hair. Let her do as she will please, I'll not go begging on my knees. I'll lock myself in tower keep, and for a while I'd moan and weep, for fortune was beyond my reach, she lives in walls I cannot breech.

Finally, when quite alone, a soul all withered, a heart of stone, I sat down sadly at my desk and began to write this picaresque. Satisfaction does it bring when quite alone to boldly sing and let your inner voice be heard. A sound there comes from a once silent bird.

Who did hear my lonely call? Who did watch as I did scrawl? To my feet fate thought to crawl.

Diversity

Many there are who, if they dared, would like my face to smack. A few in there would go too far and wish my skull would crack.

They would say I earned as much, for morals I do lack. What can I do? Fed a diet from the world of blatant, brazen sin, my arteries are restricted by a sturdy moral plaque.

But I'm not some kind of cruel and heartless psycho maniac. Most of my life was dull enough, I stayed upon the tracks. Little I had to carry round, it would barely fill a sack. Worry I did, most of the time, of the shirt upon my back. Would I lose it suddenly to fate's unseen attack?

I haven't lived to please the hoard, they're fickle and they're vain, behaviours well established in a world that's gone insane. I feel I live upon a very different moral plane. Simple are my principles, easy to attain. Let others do as they will do, so long as they won't cause pain.

It's politic to join the crowd upon their moral train, and fit in just as best you can where puritans do reign. Please excuse me, I'm not going there, I think I will abstain. I like the colours in the world, I find just white arcane. I want a world of freedom. In this there's much to gain.

Hope

I've lived and I've loved and I've lost. Fate demands an immeasurable cost. What she gives out with the right is quickly taken by her left, and not in equal parts, often leaving us bereft of the means by which we seek, from our desperate situation, atrophied and weak, to alleviate the suffering descended from above. Into our grave we fear we'll fall with the slightest of fate's shove.

But hope you can, and hope you will, cause hope is life's most potent pill. Pandora, known to toy with locks, had an enigmatic box, and sure enough she opened wide the world to that from which we'd hide, the evil and the misery, Nuck's sustained artillery. But with it came our last salvation, the thread we cling to, all creation, solace in our times of need, one last crumb on which to feed, a feeling we can't live without, fastened firmly, strong and stout, which all the souls are sure to sprout, that with which we cannot cope, our inextinguishable hope.

Meagre rations, you might say, to keep the wolf of death at bay. Hold fast to this last vestige from the light when trapped in Nuck's perplexing plight. When we feel that all is lost, beset by fate's indifferent frost, do not let go this final rope, an fairie sent, eternal hope.

Children

March! An hour at a time, as though escaping from a crime. The crime your birth, and since that day you've wasted all the hours away. And what will happen? Soon you'll die. A fact you surely won't deny. How, then, can you leave your mark within a world so filled with dark?

Chances there are all around, a king you'll be without a crown if with the children you will play. Fairie tales, a cart, a sleigh, draughts or chess, a ball you throw, perhaps a game of tic tac toe. Through children is the whole world lit, to them alone will Nuck submit.

From State we've had our children taught. Obedience is what they've sought. To raise us as a race of slaves, to punish when we misbehave. But this is not just what we want. Our souls are shrivelled, starved and gaunt. Emerging from our State run cult, not one of us has grown adult.

Adult is freedom, pure and plain. But freedom that's been yoked with reins. Principles we hold to fast. Morals forged, in iron cast. Rules we write, we choose ourselves, an order to our moral shelves.

Not imposed from high above, not inflicted with a shove, but chosen carefully, out of love.

Some may say most men are bad, so straighten out the little lad. We'll clean him up and and make him work, one day he'll serve as the perfect clerk. I say the chains on him we place will send the honest child berserk.

Listen, then, to what he thinks. He's out of line? Don't make a stink. Don't train him from your hand to shrink. From your hand he should expect a patient, measured, true respect. This can produce the desired effect. Treat well the future's architect.

Law

Man evolved a hand from paw and set that hand to writing law. At first our men did pass the test, seeking laws that served us best. Those men are gone, and in their place we've put a sadly selfish race. Preening feathers, beating chest, popular their only quest, their only merit, only aim. What a shame, the way we've structured this important game.

Each new leader, he or she, hopes for immortality. Achieves, he will, this state of grace, when law is but a piece of lace he wears to decorate his face. So write, he does, at a furious pace, as immortality his name does chase.

What have we now? An endless book, as government our freedoms took away from us, by one but one, until that freedom's all but done. Each new rule these fools do write, from our freedom takes a bite. Under his persistent eye, behaviour he will codify until his name in lights does shine, he cares not how the law confines.

Leadership is not a game meant for one to embellish his name. The laws are passed on all of us, and thus with caution and much fuss each new law we should discuss. Limited the law should be, and subject to our inquiry. Challenged often, often won, these laws must also be undone if they are found to me misplaced, if they offend the modern taste. For law is living, breathing too, A law for me may not fit you. Each case is special, each one unique. Each neighbourhood's a legal boutique. The residents quite free to critique a law they see as false antique.

I leave to you the burden, then, of laws to change, of how and when. I suggest you strike down nine in ten, and try your best to find wise men to wield the almighty legal pen.

Printed in the USA
CPSIA information can be obtained
at www.ICGtesting.com
CBHW030921140724
11443CB00027B/99